The crack of the rifle splintered the cool night air. One huge male kangaroo stumbled, then fell in a heap of askew hind legs and sinuous tail, blood spurting deep red in the beam of the spotlight.

"Got him!" the shooter exulted, raising one arm high.

Concealed by the night, the motorcycle had been able to approach closely. The rider straddled the machine, carefully sighting through a nightscope.

It was a lighter, sharper sound, but the result was the same. Blood burst from the man's throat. He seemed to hang, astonished, for a moment, then he fell with a flaccid thud.

"Got him," said the rider, the words a whisper in the darkness.

LOOKING FOR NAIAD?

Buy our books at
www.naiadpress.com

or call our toll-free number
1-800-533-1973

or by fax (24 hours a day)
1-850-539-9731

SET UP

THE 11TH DETECTIVE INSPECTOR CAROL ASHTON MYSTERY

CLAIRE McNAB

THE NAIAD PRESS, INC.
1999

Printed in the United States of America on acid-free paper
First Edition

Editor: Lila Empson
Cover designer: Bonnie Liss (Phoenix Graphics)
Typesetter: Sandi Stancil

Library of Congress Cataloging-in-Publication Data

McNab, Claire.
    Set up / Claire McNab.
        p.   cm. — (The 11th Detective Inspector Carol Ashton mystery)
    ISBN 1-56280-255-0   (alk. paper)
    1. Ashton, Carol (Fictitious character)—Fiction.   2.
Policewomen—Australia—Fiction.   3.
Lesbians—Australia—Fiction. I. Title.   II. Series: McNab, Claire.
Detective Inspector Carol Ashton mystery; 11.
PS3563.C3877S47   1999
813'.54—dc21   98-48231
                                                                      CIP

For Sheila

Acknowledgments

My thanks to my wonderful editor, Lila Empson, and to the exceptional Sandi Stancil, a typesetter who can accomplish miracles.

ABOUT THE AUTHOR

CLAIRE McNAB is the author of eleven Detective Inspector Carol Ashton mysteries: *Lessons in Murder, Fatal Reunion, Death Down Under, Cop Out, Dead Certain, Body Guard, Double Bluff, Inner Circle, Chain Letter, Past Due* and *Set Up*. She has written two romances, *Under the Southern Cross* and *Silent Heart*, and has co-authored a self-help book, *The Loving Lesbian*, with Sharon Gedan. Claire's next book will be *Murder Undercover*, the first Denise Cleever thriller.

In her native Australia she is known for her crime fiction, plays, children's novels and self-help books.

Now permanently resident in Los Angeles, Claire teaches fiction writing in the UCLA Extension Writers' Program. She makes it a point to return to Australia once a year to refresh her Aussie accent.

PROLOGUE

"There they are! Get the light on them!"

The glaring spotlight veered wildly as the four-wheel drive lurched over the rough ground. Roaring and bucking, the vehicle shuddered to a stop. In blind panic the mob of gray kangaroos began to bound in all directions, little joeys not in the pouch struggling to keep up.

Leaning on the shooting bar welded as an arch over the driver and passenger seats, the man swore as he tried to sight his heavy gun. The crack of the rifle splintered the cool night air. One huge male kangaroo stumbled, then fell in a heap of askew hind legs and sinuous tail, blood spurting deep red in the beam of the spotlight.

"Got him!" the shooter exulted, raising one arm high.

Concealed by the night and the straining engine of the four-wheel drive, the motorcycle had been able to approach closely. The rider straddled the machine, carefully sighting through a nightscope.

It was a lighter, sharper sound, but the result was the same. Blood burst from the man's throat. He seemed to hang, astonished, for a moment, then he fell with a flaccid thud into the back of the vehicle.

"Got him," said the rider, the words a whisper in the darkness.

CHAPTER ONE

Over his steepled fingers, the headmaster's expression was a nice mixture of gravity and implacability. "Your son is one of five boys suspended whilst we investigate fully. I'm afraid if our initial findings are upheld, David will be expelled."

Carol looked over at her ex-husband. In the years since they had divorced, Justin had become one of the top echelon of Sydney barristers, and with his success his once lean frame had become sleek from good living. His disarming manner had also changed with his fortunes. These days he had the manner of one accustomed to being treated as a VIP, someone whose words were listened to and given close consideration. The setting — dark paneled walls and shelves full of leather-bound books — would be familiar to him, but not the situation, where for once he was so clearly at a disadvantage.

"But, surely," Justin said in the deep, resonant voice that mesmerized witnesses and juries alike, "the school's actions are rather precipitate."

The slick leather of his chair creaked as he leaned forward to add persuasively, "I see no pressing reason for my son to be suspended at this point. His studies will be adversely affected. I understand rules, of course, but perhaps some latitude . . ."

The headmaster's severe expression didn't alter. "Mr. Hart, be assured we would not be taking these steps if there was not the strongest evidence that David has not only brought marijuana into the school for personal use, but has also, I'm very much afraid, provided the drug to other students."

He glanced at Carol. "Inspector Ashton, I'm sure you're aware that I've put the whole matter into the hands of the authorities."

Late yesterday afternoon Carol had received an embarrassed call from the officer in charge of the police station closest to the school. "Of course," she said. "I quite understand that was a step you felt you had to take."

Justin frowned. "I do think, if you'll allow me to dissent, that this has been blown completely out of proportion." He spread his hands. "I mean —*marijuana*? It's not heroin, for God's sake!"

"Our school has a no-tolerance-to-drugs policy. I cannot make exceptions." The headmaster put his

4

hands palms down on his desk, obviously about to rise and signal the end of the interview.

Carol stood first. "Thank you for seeing us at such short notice. You understand, of course, that we are both very disturbed at the accusation."

The headmaster permitted himself a faint smile. "Indeed. And I suspect that David is, at this moment, feeling even worse than his parents."

Outside the sumptuous office, Justin paused to check his appearance in a mirror. Positioning the knot of his silk tie, he said over his shoulder, "You're looking good, Carol."

"Thanks."

He half smiled at her dry tone. "I mean it. You've got style. No one would take you for a cop."

"I presume you mean that as a compliment?"

"I do." Justin nodded to the middle-aged woman sitting primly behind a mahogany desk, and strode for the door. Outside in the carpeted hall he said, "Carol, I expect you to handle the police side."

"Handle?"

He swung around to face her. "I'm not going to have my son charged over this petty issue."

"He's *our* son, Justin. And no, I'm not going to pull strings. If David's been stupid enough to do this, he should face up to the consequences."

Color rose in her ex-husband's face. "You're a police inspector, for Christ's sake! It'd just take a phone call or two. You want the media to get hold of this? They'll have a field day."

Carol gave a small grunt of amusement. "Only if there's nothing better to run with. We can just hope there's some breaking scandal that'll deflect attention."

"Carol, it's for your good as well as David's to hush things up."

"And the Justin Hart name? That wouldn't be an issue?"

He glared at her, then, as his expression altered to a reluctant grin, she saw a flash of the charm that had once captivated her.

"You're probably right," he said. "There're any number of people in the legal fraternity who'd be delighted to take me down a peg or two. Now, what are we going to do about David? I tried to talk with him last night but got nowhere. Eleanor says that I'm too hard on him."

Eleanor was Justin's second wife, a delightful woman whom Carol held in high regard. Carol had often felt a pang of envy at the bond between Eleanor and David, but she was always thankful that Justin had chosen such a fine person to be David's step-mother.

Carol said, "I'd like David to spend the weekend with me."

"The mother's touch?" There was a suggestion of a sneer in Justin's voice. Then he looked contrite. "I'm sorry. This has really got to me. David's been no trouble before this. A dream to bring up." He grimaced. "And now, on top of everything else, we have to find another suitable school for him. That may be difficult, under the circumstances."

Carol knew that by *suitable school* Justin meant an exclusive, expensive, private boys' school that had the right cachet in the circles of power. "We could enroll him in a public school," she said, aware that this would be anathema to her ex-husband.

"Of course you're joking." He slid back the sleeve

6

of his elegant suit to consult his gold watch. "I'm due in court in half an hour. Make the arrangements with Eleanor about seeing David, will you? She's coming your way tomorrow morning, so she can drop him off at your place."

In the parking lot, Carol looked at his retreating back with wry irritation. She was sure Justin was just as shaken as she was with David's transgressions. She was also convinced that David wouldn't realize the deep concern his father was feeling, but would only see the surface anger.

Justin waved to her as he pulled out in his maroon Jag. Carol paused to enjoy a moment of peaceful silence. Sheltered from the wind, the winter sunshine had such warmth that the tailored blue woolen suit she was wearing was almost too heavy for the day. She looked around, enjoying the beautifully landscaped grounds. The area where she stood was reserved for the principal and visiting guests, and Carol's plain sedan looked out of place next to the expensive vehicles. Driving in she'd noticed that the teachers and general staff were banished to a lot far from the ivy-covered main building and that their transportation was mostly as utilitarian as hers.

Before getting into the car, she flicked open her mobile phone. "I'm on the way in. Anything?"

"I'm just back from the Banning postmortem," said Mark Bourke. "Looks like it could have been a hit. Two shots from a twenty-two to the base of the skull. Hollow-point rounds that turned his brain to porridge."

"Oh *great*. I was hoping it'd be an easy one."

Laughing at her disgust, Bourke added, "And that isn't the worst of it. The super's been looking for you to do your bit for public relations. seems there's some journalist who's keen to interview you for an article."

"Why me? How about you, Mark? You can take my place. I know you'll say all the right things."

"Sorry," he said, "but it's female cops this one wants. Women in the service, and all that."

Carol made a face. She had three unsolved murders on her slate and didn't have time to worry about PR for the NSW Police Service, however much it was needed since the last adverse findings by the Police Integrity Commission. "How about Anne? She'd be perfect."

Detective Constable Anne Newsome would be an ideal subject for a positive interview. She was young, keen, and showed great promise. She also had cool good sense and could be relied on not to say anything that would embarrass the police commissioner.

Carol was congratulating herself on the suitability of her suggestion when Mark said, "Good try, Carol, but it has to be you. It's for some international piece on top women cops."

Driving through thick Friday morning traffic, Carol dismissed the minor inconvenience of some lightweight journalist to concentrate on the day ahead. Yesterday morning the wife of a high-powered businessman, Walter Banning, had found her husband slumped in the front seat of his silver Rolls-Royce. He'd been shot in the head and died instantly. The car keys were in the ignition, the engine was purring, the garage door was open. Nothing had been taken from the Rolls or the body, not even the wad of money that stuffed Banning's wallet. The Rolex had remained on his wrist and the diamond pinkie ring on his left hand. Apparently no one had heard or seen anything, and Carol had a premonition that this was going to a long, difficult case.

Generally one looked to the deceased's nearest and dearest, as there was nothing quite like close personal relationships to generate hatred and resentment. This cool murder had apparently been carefully planned, and would therefore be for a specific advantage or gain. It was too early to have firm information, but Carol was expecting that the gossip that Banning had been unfaithful in his marriage had some truth to it. If so, Banning's wife automatically would become a suspect in his death.

Perhaps Felicity Banning had a lover who'd been persuaded to remove the troublesome husband. Perhaps she'd hired a professional to do the deed. Carol shrugged to herself. Whatever she uncovered, this was a messy case with a high-profile victim who'd been the head of a multinational company, Banning & Cardover. Quite apart from the wife, there would be any number of associates to interview, and no doubt many of them would be likely to have reasons to remove him.

Banning, even in the world of ruthless business practices, had been notable for his ferocity in deal making. His partner, Cardover, a much older man, had recently been incapacitated by a stroke, but he'd played a nonactive role in the company for some years and there was no suggestion that his illness had precipitated a power struggle of any kind.

Carol swore to herself. The way things were

shaping up, there was no way she could devote the whole weekend to her son. And David would resent the fact that she had to work at least part of the time. She sighed. If only Sybil were there to pick up the slack. If only.

CHAPTER TWO

Superintendent Edgar waylaid Carol before she could get to her desk. "Carol! Step into my office for a moment, will you?"

He settled his bulk into his chair, waving her to another. "The Banning case coming along, is it?"

Keeping to herself the pulse of irritation his breezy question caused, she said, "It's very early. The postmortem was only done this morning."

"Quite. I don't need to remind you that this one's a hot potato." He tapped a tattoo with his thick fingers. "And the Fader murder?"

His query concerned the death of an automobile mechanic, found fatally beaten in his workshop after a struggle with an assailant. Carol said, "We're waiting for DNA evidence, but I'm confident we'll be arresting the brother."

"And that homeless woman?"

"Nicola Bratt." Carol pronounced the victim's name with emphasis. She'd been a nobody alive, a wraith who wandered the edges of society, but Carol was determined that her death would be treated with as much respect and attention as anyone else's would be.

Edgar nodded dismissively. "Yes, her. Nothing there, I suppose. Probably knifed by some other street person, eh?"

Carol agreed with his offhand comment, aware that the likelihood of solving this particular murder was slight. There was no weapon, Nicola Bratt had been lying for days in bushes on an abandoned lot and no relatives or friends had come forward to claim the body or to give information of her movements in the days before she was stabbed. She had been identified by an old driver's license and other papers she'd kept neatly folded and tucked into a stained money belt she'd worn under layers of mismatched clothing.

Carol said, "We've still making inquiries."

He grunted with tart amusement. "Good luck!"

The superintendent had a head of thick white hair, of which he was inordinately proud, and a handsome, fleshy face that usually held, at least to Carol, an infuriating expression of self-satisfaction. Carol knew her own face showed polite attention, not revealing the growing contempt she felt. She'd worked with the superintendent for years and was quite accustomed to his attention to self-interest. When there was trouble, he adroitly sidestepped. When accolades were to be given out, suddenly he was front and center.

For a long time she'd ignored the super's foibles, but now it was more personal, as word had got back to her that he would actively oppose her promotion to chief inspector, should she decide to apply for consideration. She was aware that he had never particularly liked her, but the real reason for his disfavor was probably rooted in her high profile in the media and her overall success rate. And it didn't help that he was a woman: Superintendent Edgar definitely belonged to the men-make-the-best-cops school of thought.

"Now, Carol," he said, fingering a business card on his desk, "there is one other thing. It seems the premier had a word with the commissioner ..." He handed her the card. "This journalist — she's a Yank, by the way — is some big deal, apparently. Can't say I've ever heard of her myself."

Carol looked at the name on the business card. "Loren Reece? I don't know the name."

Edgar waved a hand. "Freelance, I think. Writes for *Newsweek, Time*, that sort of thing." His tone made it clear these were not magazines that engaged his interest. "Whatever, she's impressed the premier for some reason, so you're to give her full cooperation. She's doing research for a series of articles on female cops in different countries, and it's an excellent opportunity for the force to make a good impression. That comes straight from the commissioner. Okay?"

"I'll try to fit her in."

Edgar sat forward. "You *will* fit her in, Carol. Good PR never hurts, and, God knows, we need it at the moment." His expression darkened. "The bloody PIC." He was referring to the latest hearings held by the Police Integrity Commission. The details of corrupt cops had garnered the usual enthusiastic media attention. "Bunch of wankers," he said, sending Carol a challenging look. "Don't you agree?"

Carol didn't. She considered the PIC a necessary evil, although recently she'd winced at the grubby revelations in the paper each morning. "Yes, we do need good PR," she said. "Is this journalist going to contact me?"

"She's going to ring for an appointment. See her as soon as you can."

Edgar brushed his palms together. It was a gesture she'd learned to read early in their professional relationship. It indicated that their conversation was over. Carol stood and, with hidden amusement, beat him to the sentence he invariably used at the close of every encounter. "I'll keep you informed," she said.

He grunted. "The Banning case is top priority," he reminded her as she reached the door.

Mark Bourke met Carol outside her office, a grin on his blunt-featured face. "Bad news," he said. "Banning's wife seems to be close to Mother Teresa in virtue. No hint of any lover keen to eliminate an awkward husband. In fact, Felicity Banning appears not only to have been devoted to her husband, but more than willing to turn a blind eye to his shenanigans."

Carol led the way into her office, its neutral walls and standard-issue furniture soothing in its bland familiarity. "How are you doing with Banning's business associates?"

"Plenty of animosity, but no motives strong enough to off the guy. I've got Maureen going through the financial records, but his company isn't involved in any contentious merger or takeover. Banning wasn't liked, but on the whole he was respected. There's the pending uranium mine development in Papua New Guinea that's been getting a lot of flack in the media, but that's fading now that concessions have been made to the environmentalists."

He folded his long body onto an uncomfortable wooden chair. "This really could be a pro working here, Carol. Amateurs make mistakes, but this is a very clean killing. Banning kisses his wife good-bye, goes down to the garage and hops into his Rolls, punches a button to open the door, someone comes in, leans though the car window and shoots him twice in the head." He tilted his head. "Efficient, wouldn't you say? No witnesses, and scene-of-crime have come up with absolutely nothing."

"Ballistics?"

He shook his head. "Don't think there'll be much joy there. When Jeff George fished the slugs out of Banning's head this morning, the slugs were deformed from bouncing around inside the skull."

Having witnessed many of the pathologist's post-mortems, Carol had a clear picture of Jeff George at work. She could imagine his cheerful patter as raised his booming voice above the whine of the bone saw. She could see him lifting off the top of Banning's skull to peer inside with all the enthusiasm of some-

15

one opening a gift. Carol had often wondered what it was in the pathologist that inured him to the work that he did. Only with children's corpses had she ever seen his vitality dampened. Usually he greeted each body with the eagerness of a puzzle-solver faced with a series of challenges.

"If it is a professional hit," said Bourke, "I'd say we look for the money. See who in Banning's circle gains a lot from his death. That'd be our best bet, I reckon."

Carol's phone rang. She gestured for him to stay as she picked up the receiver. "Carol Ashton."

"Inspector, my name's Loren Reece. You may have been told I'd call." The voice was pleasantly American, with a light accent that Carol couldn't categorize as coming from any particular part of the States.

"It was mentioned to me."

A soft chuckle came down the line. "And I'm sure, Inspector, that you're very busy, and not altogether thrilled with the idea of an interview."

"Ms. Reece —"

"Please call me Loren. I was wondering if next Tuesday would fit in with your schedule?"

Carol made a face at Bourke, who was grinning at her exasperated expression. "Next Tuesday?" she said, hunting around on her desk for her appointment diary. "Please hold for a moment."

Putting her hand over the receiver, she said to Bourke, "I really don't need this."

He fished her diary out from under a pile of papers and handed it to her. "Although you hide it well," he said, "I can tell you bask in all this media attention."

16

Carol flipped over to Tuesday and stared glumly at the page. Removing her hand from the mouthpiece, she said, "Ms. Reece?"

"Loren."

"I can see you Tuesday morning at ten. You know the address here?"

"I have your location, thanks. I was rather hoping I could take you to lunch."

Carol glared at the phone. "I'm sorry," she said, "but I'm afraid that's impossible."

Apparently not at all put out by Carol's cool tone, the American said cheerfully, "Ten it is, on Tuesday. I look forward to it, Inspector."

As Carol put down the phone, Constable Goolwa put his head through the door. "Inspector? I'm sorry to interrupt, but there's something on the Nicola Bratt case."

She waved the young constable in, a little amused at his diffidence. Sam Goolwa had only been on her team for a few weeks, and was still feeling his way. His Aboriginal heritage had given him a lean, resilient frame, crinkled dark hair and eyes of such a deep brown that they were almost black. European blood had lightened the rich color of his skin to a satiny tan.

"We've got a suspect," he said. "Matthew Bott's his name. Got drunk and smashed up a Salvation Army homeless shelter last night. When he was arrested, he started raving about this woman he said he'd stabbed. Had a knife on him that fits the murder weapon. He's up for drunk and disorderly, but he could be our man."

"Bott's still in custody?"

When Goolwa nodded, she said, "Okay, I'll leave it
to you and Anne to handle it." She didn't miss the
look of pleasure that flashed across his face. "Keep me
informed," she said, inwardly smiling that she was
parroting Superintendent Edgar's customary admoni-
tion.

After Goolwa had gone, Bourke said, "He'll do
okay. Have to toughen up a bit, develop a thicker skin,
but he's got what it takes."

There were comparatively few Aborigines in the
Police Service, and Carol was aware that prejudices
still lingered from the bad old days. "Is he having
trouble with anyone in particular?"

"Nothing he can't handle." Bourke's tone made it
clear he didn't think Carol should interfere. He leaned
forward to fish his wallet out of his hip pocket. "Want
to see another couple of pictures of Carli?"

Pat, Bourke's wife, had recently had their first
child, a little girl, and Bourke had become as besotted
a father as Carol had ever seen.

Carol put out her hand. "Do I have a choice?" she
asked, laughing.

"Well, you *are* Carli's godmother."

Carol had been surprised and, astonishing herself,
ridiculously pleased when she'd been asked to be the
baby's godmother. And Carli had been an exemplary
infant, gurgling happily through her baptism and
bestowing a toothless smile on anyone who came close
to her.

Carol's phone shrilled. "This better not be another
journalist."

After a short conversation, she replaced the
receiver and gave Bourke an interrogative look. "What

18

do you think of this? Banning's partner, Cardover, died this morning."

"Natural causes? He'd had a stroke."

"Seems to be."

"Interesting timing," said Bourke.

CHAPTER THREE

Wallhaven, the very expensive private hospital where Eric Cardover had died, was located in an upscale suburban setting, its bland facade, ordered gardens and closely mowed grass so similar to its anonymous neighbors that at first glance it was just a very large house. Carol had the whimsical thought that if the building had been a human suspect, the face would have been instantly forgettable.

Carol had decided that she and Bourke would carry

out the inquiry, even though it seemed a basic matter that only required a junior officer to accomplish.

"I've got a feeling about this convenient death, Mark. Not a good feeling," she'd said in her office. Now, looking at the undistinguished entrance to the hospital, she felt another prickle of apprehension.

"I'm sure the death certificate is already signed," she said to Bourke, "but if anything looks the slightest suspicious, I want a post."

Bourke had alerted Cardover's supervising doctor, and he was waiting for them in a heavily carpeted, neutral-toned office that was as insipid as the building itself.

"Mr. Cardover died early this morning," he said without ceremony, once the introductions were over. Retreating behind a large desk, he continued, "There was no mystery about it, and I've signed the death certificate. Frankly, I'm not altogether clear how I can help you."

Dr. Olson had a balding head that seemed too large for his diminutive body. His features were small and sharp, and he fidgeted with the papers on the desk as he spoke. "All our patients receive the very best medical care, but Mr. Cardover had suffered a massive stroke two months ago that left him almost totally incapacitated."

"Was he conscious?"

Dr. Olson frowned at Carol's question. "If you mean did he respond to outside stimuli, then, yes, there had been improvement since he became our patient." He picked up a stack of papers and tapped them on the desktop to align them. "Mr. Cardover's stroke was so severe that he had very little physical

21

movement remaining and he couldn't speak. He drifted in and out of consciousness, but he was making appreciable progress and I anticipated that he would recover further."

Bourke said, "Was his death a surprise to you?"

"Not at all. There was always a chance of a further stroke. In the end, his heart simply stopped."

"Was any attempt made to resuscitate him?" asked Carol.

Dr. Olson fussed with the positioning of the papers. "No heroic measures are indicated with a patient in Mr. Cardover's condition. And he had made his wishes clear on this matter some time before his illness. His family concurred."

"Is his body still in the hospital?"

Twisting his mouth as if he found Bourke's question in poor taste, he said, "His family made the arrangements. I believe the funeral directors are Ballard and Coombe. They collected the remains this morning."

"We'd like to interview the staff on duty when he died."

"Surely that's not necessary, Inspector. We provide the most excellent medical care." A querulous note entered his voice as he added, "The man died because he'd had a catastrophic stroke. Simple as that."

"Have you heard that his partner, Walter Banning, was murdered yesterday morning?" said Bourke.

"Yes, I know that, but it can have nothing to do with Mr. Cardover dying." His indignant expression changed to one of concern. "You can't be suggesting there's any connection between the two!"

"It's just a matter of tying up a loose end," said Carol soothingly.

Dr. Olson looked at her with suspicion. "Oh, really?" he said, his tone caustic. "Detective Inspector Ashton has time to tie up a loose end here and there? I don't believe it."

Carol smiled at him. "Just keeping my hand in."

Eric Cardover had been looked after by a rotation of three nurses who had been scheduled to tend to him exclusively. The nurse who had been on duty when he died had just returned to the hospital to work another shift, so Carol asked Dr. Olson to arrange for her to meet them in the room where Cardover had died. The doctor took them upstairs himself, all the while explaining how Wallhaven Hospital provided superior care and how its security arrangements were second to none. Carol thought wryly that the man had every reason to be concerned that the family of the deceased might get wind of tho investigation and threaten to sue for negligence.

The second floor of the building was not quite as sterile as most hospitals were. Care had been taken to choose agreeable artworks, all in pastels with nothing to jar the eye. The central nurses' station was done in white and turquoise, and the staff hurried around in uniforms of the same colors. An adjacent waiting area was thickly carpeted, with furniture that appeared expensive and floral arrangements that were fresh.

Dr. Olson led them down a wide white corridor to the end room. Carol wrinkled her nose at the faint smell of polish and disinfectant mingled with the scent of flowers. Even blindfolded, she was sure she would always recognize a hospital by those pervasive odors.

Olson said, "This is the room." To one side of the wide white door was a red exit sign and a doorway that obviously led to a stairway.

"Fire stairs?" said Carol.

Olson nodded and ushered them into Cardover's room. It was flooded with pitiless light from the large window, which looked out onto the neat gardens and entrance driveway. There was an adjoining private bathroom. The furniture was modern and sleek, but the hospital bed was the usual utilitarian unit. The sheets and blankets had already been stripped, although equipment, including a heart monitor, still sat next to the head of the bed. Carol thought that there must have been flowers and personal items to brighten the cold formality of the room, but, if so, these had all disappeared. Any sign that a person with hopes and fears had occupied the bed had been wiped away.

Nurse Slade was a bluff, no-nonsense woman with a rigid back and an abrupt manner. "Mr. Cardover died this morning at five-thirty." Her iron-gray hair was as stiff as the starched uniform she wore. Carol fleetingly thought that turquoise was not the nurse's best color.

"You were with him at the time?" said Bourke.

Nurse Slade looked over at Olson, then back to Bourke. "Not at the exact moment."

"Where were you?"

She took immediate offense at Bourke's question. "I wasn't neglecting my patient, if that's what you're implying. I went to get a coffee, just a few steps away."

Carol indicated the monitor and other equipment. "I presume an alarm alerted you that something was wrong."

A frown creased the nurse's forehead. "Not exactly. I was out of the room for a few moments, and when I came back I found he'd gone."

"There was no alert at the nurses' station?" Dr. Olson was scandalized at this failure. He turned to Carol and Bourke. "I assure you our equipment is regularly tested." A gimlet look at Nurse Slade followed. "You didn't report any malfunction," he snapped.

She straightened, obviously annoyed. "Because there *was* no malfunction. When I checked right after Mr. Cardover died, I found the power to the machines had become disconnected. Up until then, it'd been working perfectly."

"It had become disconnected?" said Carol. "By itself?"

"Look," said Nurse Slade with a militant glare, "it wouldn't have made one bit of difference. A cleaner, perhaps, pulled the lead loose, or maybe it wasn't in tightly enough." She continued with an air of one vindicated. "There was a do-not-resuscitate on my patient, so even if the alarm had sounded, Mr. Cardover would be, if you don't mind me saying it, just as dead. It was only a matter of time."

"Exactly how long were you away from the room?"

Nurse Slade lifted her shoulders. "I don't know. Five minutes, perhaps."

"Could it have been longer?"

Carol's question brought an exasperated sigh. "I wasn't watching the time. Mr. Cardover was resting quietly, and I went to get something to drink. I may have been four minutes, or six minutes. I can't tell you precisely."

"Did you see anyone near Mr. Cardover's room?"

25

Her momentary look of surprise was followed by a wary expression. "There are always people around in a hospital."

Carol was sure Nurse Slade was not being entirely open. "You did see something, didn't you?"

"Not really."

"A cleaner?" asked Bourke. When Nurse Slade frowned at him, he added, "You said perhaps a cleaner inadvertently disconnected the monitor."

She hesitated, then said, "I was walking back with one of the other nurses. We were talking, and I glanced in this direction and caught a glimpse of someone near Mr. Cardover's room."

"Male or female?"

Carol's question clearly irritated Nurse Slade. "It was a glimpse, I said. I just saw the white coat and blue pants. That's what orderlies at Wallhaven wear. Could have been a man or a woman. I've no idea."

Bourke asked, "Where did this person go?"

"Through the exit door and down the stairs, I imagine. Are you suggesting there's something suspicious about Mr. Cardover's death?"

Olson blanched. "Impossible. Absolutely impossible."

Carol felt a twinge of sympathy for the man. "I'm sorry," she said, "but there'll have to be a postmortem on Mr. Cardover's body."

"If you don't need me further," said Nurse Slade, "I'll get back to my patients."

Carol indicated the bare bed. "Can you tell me where the bedclothes are now?"

"Gone to the laundry. His towel, everything." The nurse seemed to take some pleasure in adding, "You'll never find them now. All the dirty linen gets dumped together."

"We'll have further questions, and will need a full statement from you," said Carol.

"I've told you all I know, but very well. When you want me, I'll be somewhere on this floor." She marched, rather than walked, out of the room.

"This room will have to be secured until we can get a crime-scene team here."

"Crime scene!" Olson's voice rose with indignation. "Inspector, I can't believe you seriously think that someone got in and murdered one of our patients. The very thought is outrageous."

"I know it's very inconvenient, but we'll try to have the room released as soon as possible." When he nodded reluctantly, Carol continued, "And it would help if we could see Nurse Slade's personnel file."

"Marilyn Slade is an excellent employee," he protested. "I've never had any complaint about her work. On the contrary, she is very highly regarded by staff and patients alike."

"Nevertheless," said Carol, "we need her file. And we'll also need details of Mr. Cardover's family, so we can contact them regarding the body. There can be no funeral until it's established how he died."

Olson seemed ready to argue, then his shoulders drooped. "If I refuse, I imagine you'll get some sort of court order, but I must say I consider this an extreme overreaction to what seems to me to be a simple problem with the alarm component of the equipment."

"Or perhaps a simple case of murder," said Bourke to Carol.

* * * * *

By late Friday afternoon Bourke had a checklist of names of all Wallhaven staff on duty on the floor where Cardover had died, and had assigned the interviewing assignment to two constables, Li and Standish.

Carol had decided to visit the grieving widow herself, in part because she was reluctant to go back to the office on such a beautiful afternoon, but mainly because she wanted to get a feel for the Cardover family.

The impeccably dressed woman Carol met had a chilly manner and a hard face. She didn't appear to have shed one tear over her husband's death. "My son, Jonathan," she said, once Carol was inside the luxurious Wollstonecraft townhouse.

Jonathan Cardover was in his forties, a blank-faced man with discontented mouth and contemptuous manner. He excused himself and left Carol and his mother alone.

Phyllis Cardover was scandalized to discover that it was likely there'd be a delay in the funeral arrangements.

"I've got people coming internationally for the service," she said sharply. "Not to mention VIPs here in Australia. Really, Inspector, this is *very* inconvenient. I expect you to inform me *immediately* when you release the body."

Carol left the Cardover townhouse in a dark mood, wondering when she died if there would be people she held dear who would be irritated at some hitch in her funeral arrangements rather than be so swamped by grief that such a problem was of no consequence. Then Carol had to grin to herself: Contemplating one's own funeral was the height of self-indulgence, especially as she'd imagined herself floating above the crowd of sorrowful friends listening to them saying laudatory things about her.

She groaned at the peak-hour traffic on the Pacific Highway. She wanted to be heading the opposite way, to her home, but instead she grimly pointed the car in the direction of the city. She didn't want to go via the Harbour Tunnel today — the late winter sun was warm and the sky washed pale blue, so she jostled her way into the stream of traffic pouring onto the Harbour Bridge. She admired the huge sandstone pylons and the gray arch of girders passing above her and, as always, she glanced over at the Opera House when she reached the city end of the bridge. From the car she could only see a portion of the soaring curved roofs, but it was a personal talisman to her, something unique and beautiful that for a moment allowed her to transcend the pressures and responsibilities of her job.

Mark Bourke was waiting. "Here's Marilyn Slade's statement," he said, handing her stapled pages. "Doesn't add anything to what she said to us, except that she's now admitting she could have been out of the room for up to fifteen minutes, which probably means twenty at least. Plenty of time for someone to sneak in and kill him."

"None of this is of any interest unless Cardover was murdered," said Carol. "Did you charm Jeff George into doing the postmortem on Monday? Cardover's widow is not a bit happy at the delay."

"Wants to get it over and done with?" said Bourke. "I'm not a bit surprised. Probably can't wait to get her hands on the millions she stands to inherit. Well, she'll have to wait. The earliest we can get Cardover done is Tuesday afternoon, and I only got that concession by begging. Quite embarrassed myself."

Carol grinned. She couldn't visualize Mark Bourke humiliating himself to plead for anything. He was one of those people who were so obviously pleasant and genuine that most people found themselves wanting to help him solve whatever problem faced him, but he could also be tough and uncompromising. Carol had seen him deal with vicious criminals with a flinty intensity that was intimidating in its concentrated focus, but usually he was disarmingly mild.

"Another thing," said Bourke. "Sam Goolwa's got a confession for the Bratt murder. I rather think he'd like to tell you about it himself."

When he came to her office, Sam Goolwa could hardly hide his keen satisfaction. "Bott came right out and confessed, Inspector. Told Anne and me what made him do it." His expression sobered. "He killed Nicola Bratt for a half-full flagon of cheap sherry."

Carol glanced through the confession. Bott claimed to have paid half the money for the flagon, but when he wanted his fair share of the alcohol, Nicola Bratt had refused to hand it over. They'd struggled, but she wouldn't let go and had started screaming for help. Bott had taken out the knife he always carried for self-defense and stabbed her until she fell. Then he had snatched up the sherry and run.

Matthew Bott had scrawled his name untidily at the bottom of the typed words. There was a smear of dirt, or sweat, where his hand had rested on the page.

"You've charged him?"

"Yes. He'll be arraigned on Monday."

"Good work, Sam."

Goolwa beamed at her, then nodded awkwardly and hurried out of her office.

Carol looked at her gold watch. It had been a gift

from Sybil. It was a delicate thing, closer to jewelry than a timepiece, and nothing that Carol would have bought for herself. With luck, Sybil would be home from teaching and Carol could tell her about David's sins.

As she punched in the numbers, Carol had a feeling that she really should have called Sybil as soon as she'd been told what David had done. Carol had contacted her Aunt Sarah immediately, but she'd put off this call for as long as she could.

"It's Carol."

"You don't have to tell me, I know your voice." Sybil sounded tired and edgy.

Prickling with the unpleasant impression that Sybil wanted her off the phone as soon as possible, Carol briefly ran through David's illicit activities.

"Carol! Has he been arrested?"

"Not exactly. He'll appear in the children's court, of course, so his name won't be released. It's his first offense, so he'll get off with a talking to and a bond. The worst thing from David's point of view, I suspect, is that he'll be expelled from his school."

"Poor David. Can I see him?"

"He's staying with me for the weekend. I was wondering if you had any time then."

"Sunday?"

"Great. I'll drop him off in the morning, if that's all right." There was an awkward pause. Carol filled it by saying, "I won't stay. I'll leave him as long as you like, then pick him up when you say."

Sybil made an amused sound. "You can stay if you like."

"Well, actually, I do have work to do."

"Another pressing case?" Sybil's voice was sardonic.

"I'll be pleased to baby-sit your son for you." Before Carol could respond, Sybil went on in a chastened tone, "I'm sorry, Carol. That wasn't fair. I'd be delighted to spend some time with my favorite young man, and I'll drive him back to Seaforth. It's no trouble."

Carol's heart rose a little. "You could look at the house. It's almost finished. Well, pretty close to finished. You'll hardly recognize the place."

"I'll recognize it," said Sybil. "I won't come in. Don't ask me to."

CHAPTER FOUR

Eleanor Hart dropped David off at Carol's Seaforth house on Saturday morning. Carol's heart always gave a small lurch when she saw her son. He had her pale blond hair and green eyes, but the set of his jaw was Justin's, and he was going to be tall and broad shouldered, like his father. Every now and then a familiar question rose unbidden in Carol's mind. What if she had fought to keep him all those years ago? Would he be a different person if she had brought him up?

She smiled a welcome to Eleanor, thinking how

kind and capable she was. Carol had to admit to herself that Justin's second wife was probably a better mother than Carol, with all the demands of her career, would have had time to be.

"Coffee?" she said, hoping to have a private word with Eleanor about David.

"Love to, Carol, but I've got to run. I've been talked into helping out a friend on an animal welfare stall in the middle of the Esplanade at Manly." Eleanor gestured toward her car, parked above in Carol's street level carport. "Brutus is in there, all dressed up with a scarf around his neck and a sign that says PLEASE HELP, and I venture no one's going to be able to resist him."

"I know I wouldn't be able to. In fact, let me make a donation right now."

"Brutus is a ham," said David, dumping his overnight bag on the ground.

"A quality that's a great help when you're collecting money," said his stepmother. "Carol, you don't need to give anything."

Brutus was an indulged golden retriever with a sweet nature and a penchant for stealing food. Carol had seen his soulful trick of cocking his head and giving a hopeful doggy smile, and could imagine that he would be spectacular in extracting cash donations from people passing by on a busy Saturday morning near the beach.

"I'll come up and say hello, then I'll have to contribute something substantial," said Carol with a laugh. "I'm a total pushover for that dog."

Brutus was delighted to see Carol, but then, he was delighted to see everyone. It was an open secret that he was the world's very worst watchdog and would be far more likely to welcome burglars than to bark at them.

Carol insisted on giving a donation, then she and David stood together to wave Eleanor off. Walking back down the sloping path to the house, David indicated an untidy pile of demolished material that had half buried a flower bed. "When are the builders going to finish? It's been going on for ages."

Carol put her hands on her hips. "Search me. It's taking longer than the estimate, and it's costing more than I expected, but veterans of alterations tell me that always happens." She surveyed the house, so changed from the comfortable old familiar dwelling she'd lived in for so many years. Flowers were trampled, temporary tin sheds held cement and supplies, and lumber was stacked on the lawn. "I have the awful feeling it'll be the million-dollar makeover by the time the builders decide it's done."

"Has Sybil seen it?"

"No."

Her detached tone didn't stop him from asking, "Is she coming back?"

"I don't think so."

David looked sideways at her. "But you did all this for Sybil, didn't you? All those changes."

"Uh-huh." This wasn't a subject she wanted to discuss, so she led the way through the front door and down the hall to the back of the house.

"Gee," said David. "It's a lot different."

Carol suddenly realized how long it had been since she'd had him home with her. She'd got into a habit of taking him out somewhere, to a movie or a sporting event, or bushwalking. A couple of times they had been up to the Blue Mountains to visit Aunt Sarah or had stayed overnight somewhere, but since Sybil had moved out for good, Carol had resisted bringing David back here.

"Where's the kitchen gone?" he asked.

"The old one's been demolished altogether, along with the living room."

Carol had a sudden vivid image of Sybil unconscious on the floor of the living room by the sofa, her wrists handcuffed, her face bruised and bleeding. After, she'd said she didn't think she could ever live in this house again, that what had happened to her there had poisoned the place.

Carol felt a prickle of indignation. It wasn't the same room, the same house — it was utterly changed. She'd even got rid of all the furniture in the living room, although she'd been fond of its clean lines. She said, "The new kitchen's where my bedroom was, and my new bedroom's over there."

She indicated an extension to the back of the house. The original wooden deck that had given such spectacular views of Middle Harbour had been extended to three sides of the house, and Carol's bedroom shared that outlook, so that she could wake and see through a huge picture window the wide expanse of water through the trees.

Black-and-white Sinker joined them with a here-I-am meow. He had shown a keen interest in every detail of the rebuilding, and he spent most of his time checking out exactly what the workmen were doing. As David bent to stroke the cat, Carol recounted how two weeks before Sinker had managed to get himself built into a section of the roof. "I came home late from work, and all I could hear were these outraged shrieks. Took me ages to work out where he was, and then I had to break down part of the ceiling to get him out."

"Poor Sinker," said David. He added innocently, "I suppose he misses Jeffrey."

Jeffrey was Sybil's cat, and Carol wasn't going to talk about that. "Sinker's fully occupied being a feline foreman for the builders," she said.

Carol and David stood shoulder to shoulder, leaning on the railing and looking down the cliff to where sailboats flirted with the wind. "How about you tell me about your career dealing in cannabis," she said.

"Aw, Mum! It wasn't like that at all. I wasn't *dealing*, not really."

"What *were* you doing?"

"A couple of the other kids in my class asked me to get it for them."

"And how did they know you could?"

David shrugged elaborately. "I dunno."

"Right," said Carol. "Let's get this straight. Certain students in your class just happen to ask you to buy marijuana for them. Out of the blue. And what a surprise! You conveniently know a source."

David gave her an unwilling smile. "Okay, Mum. It wasn't quite like that. I'm on the junior soccer team at school with this guy, and I guess he told some of the others that I could get the stuff."

"How would he know that?"

"It's his older brother who gave it to me."

"*Gave* it. How generous."

David winced at her sarcasm. "Okay, so he sold it to me."

"Is this brother a student at your school?"

"Left a few years ago."

Carol turned to face him. "His name?"

David gave her a small grin. "Smith, actually."
Seeing her expression, he protested, "It *is*"

"Smith?" Carol's tone was dry. "And I suppose his
first name is John?"

"Nope. Paul. And the guy in my class is Pete."

Carol glared at him. This was like getting blood
out of a stone, and David was exhibiting a cocky non-
chalance that infuriated her. "Why didn't your friend
Pete sell his brother's cannabis?" she asked, trying to
keep her tone reasonable.

"Pete? Too scared, so he asked me to do it."

"And you, like a fool, agreed."

David pushed out his bottom lip, suddenly looking
years younger. "It was no big deal," he said. "Like it
wasn't anything *hard*."

"Of course it's a big deal. I can't even begin to
imagine why you were so stupid. Didn't you think
about what would happen if you got caught."

"It was just for fun."

"It's very far from fun. What you did was illegal,
and you knew it was." He opened his mouth to reply,
but she gestured for him to be quiet. "And don't tell
me marijuana is a soft drug and lots of people break
the law and smoke it. That isn't the point. In terms
of the law, you're a drug dealer. How does that
sound?"

"I didn't think —"

"You certainly didn't. Now, just for once, use your
brains. When you make your statement to the police,
you are going to name names, David. Everyone who
had anything to do with this."

"I'm not a dobber. There's no way I'm telling on
my friends."

His truculent statement made her want to shake

him, hard. She took a deep breath. "I am so furious with you, David. In my wildest dreams I could never imagine you doing something like this."

He shuffled his feet, hands jammed in his pockets. "You sound just like Dad."

"That's because your father and I agree entirely on this subject."

She looked at his bent head with exasperated anger. Where was the little child who'd once been so full of uncomplicated enthusiasm? The boy who'd grown into a rather serious kid who played sport well and whose academic results were mostly good?.

With an effort she swallowed her anger. "Come on, we'll collect wood for the barbecue and you can cook us a couple of steaks for lunch. Okay?"

His look of surprise at her mild tone almost made her smile. "I'm still going to yell at you later," she said. "A lot. You can count on that."

As they were going into the house the phone rang. Carol glanced at her watch. Aunt Sarah was right on time. Carol had received an e-mail from her aunt yesterday demanding to know when and where she could speak with David. Carol could visualize her in her cottage in the Blue Mountains, staring at her computor monitor, then stabbing at the keyboard with two fingers. The electronic communication revolution had not passed Aunt Sarah by. On the contrary, she had embraced the new technology with her typical enthusiasm, and Carol was accustomed to receiving a barrage of comments, questions and advice via e-mail.

She picked up the phone in the kitchen, said hello to her aunt, then handed the receiver to David. "It's Aunt Sarah for you."

Twenty minutes later he came outside looking subdued. When she asked a few mild questions, he mumbled that they'd talked about nothing much.

"I had to tell her about it," Carol said.

He kicked at the ground. "I suppose," he said dolefully.

In the late afternoon Carol collected her neighbor's German shepherd and went for a run with David through the bushland near Carol's house. Olga, after a few overjoyed barks to show her appreciation of this unexpected outing, loped ahead of them with such natural grace that Carol felt awkward, even though she was running with practiced ease.

The dirt paths skirting the edge of the cliff were deserted, and a crisp wind blew up from the gray-green water of the harbor. Previously Carol had been able to outpace her son, but David had grown taller and stronger during the last year, and he forged ahead of her, scrambling over the rough places and splashing through the puddles left from last night's rain.

The sudden downpour just after midnight had woken Carol, and she hadn't been able to go back fully to sleep for hours. She'd half dozed, her thoughts running in circles: David and what he'd done; the cases she was working on; what she should say to Sybil when they met on Sunday morning. About two-thirty she got up, put on a warm dressing gown, and boiled milk in the half-built kitchen. The smell of sawdust and the adhesive used to glue the new bench tops in place filled the room and Carol had looked around, trying to visualize it finished and gleaming.

Sinker had been delighted to find that she was up, making it clear that he had serious intentions of inveigling a snack from her. It had been easier to shut him up with food, so she'd given him his breakfast four hours early. Finding some ancient cocoa in the back of a cupboard, she'd stirred a generous quantity into the hot milk and then had sat pensively gazing at her reflection in the sliding glass doors that led to the deck.

The storm had slacked off, and the rain pattering against the roof and the leaves of the eucalyptus gums crowding the back of the house made a pleasant noise, but the outside chill crept into the kitchen, and Carol shivered. Unwillingly, she thought about Nicola Bratt, and all the street people like her. Individuals who had no homes, no secure shelter from the weather. What could have happened in Nicola's life to send her to live a mean existence on the unfeeling streets of Sydney? Carol knew that a high proportion of homeless people had problems with alcohol or drugs. Many suffered untreated mental illness or severe personality problems. But still, Carol thought, there had to be that one moment when Nicola Bratt knew that she no longer could have a normal life. Or perhaps it wasn't a clear recognition of how her existence had changed, but was rather a slow decline until she found herself scavenging for food and begging for money, hardly knowing how she had come to this pass. And to be murdered for a half-flagon of cheap sherry.

Carol had gone back to bed chilled not only by the cold but also by her thoughts. The warm milk, however, had done its work, exactly as her mother had always said it would when Carol couldn't sleep when a child. Carol had fallen into a deep and dreamless sleep, and had the luxury of a couple of extra hours, as she knew she would have her daily run in the afternoon with her son.

She smiled at David's back as he picked up the pace. The path had become even rougher, degraded by heavy winter rains, so it was hard to keep up their former speed. "You're getting old, Mum," David called out over his shoulder. Then he skidded as his feet slid on a patch of dark mud, and he landed on his nose.

Laughing, Carol helped him up, assisted by Olga, who had come back to see what was happening. "The old saying, pride goes before a fall, applies here, I believe."

His teeth were white in his muddy face. "I guess."

He brushed off what mud he could, then they walked on until they came to one of Carol's favorite places, a rocky promontory that jutted out over Middle Harbour. The air was full of the delicious scent of damp earth and wet eucalyptus leaves. With her usual enthusiasm, Olga went foraging for prey. This was a hopeless enterprise, as in all the times Carol had been with her in the bush, Olga had never succeeded in running anything to ground. In fact, in spring Olga always had the embarrassment of having nesting magpies dive-bombing her head when she came too close.

Carol, realizing that her son would soon be taller than she, put an arm around his shoulders. The sunset was a spectacular orange-red band, illuminating the bottoms of high clouds with a ruddy glow. Far to the west, over the convoluted shores of Middle Harbour, they could see the skeleton outlines of television broadcast towers.

"Beautiful, isn't it?" said Carol, elated to share the

moment with someone she cared about. She rarely felt lonely, but being with David was an uncomfortable reminder of how much richer life could be.

"Not bad," he said. "I'm cold. I'll race you back."

CHAPTER FIVE

Sunday morning was windy and cold, but glaringly sunny too. Shredded clouds scudded across the sky, and the trees thrashed in the stiff breeze. David sat beside Carol and played with the controls of her car radio, apparently with the ambition of deafening her with the loudest pop music he could find.

They were driving the wild bush area of Wakehurst Parkway and were halfway to Sybil's house before he spoke. Snapping off a particularly irritating song that featured the lead singer lamenting in a nasal dirge the loss of his only true love, David said, "I really won't have to leave school, will I, Mum?"

Carol glanced at his serious face. "I think you will."

"But Dad can fix it, can't he? The headmaster will listen to him."

"I doubt your dad can do anything. It's a strict school rule. No drugs."

"It's a stupid rule! I could tell you about other guys who've done it, and they aren't being kicked out."

"This isn't about other guys. This is about you."

He slumped in the seat. "But all my friends are there, and I'm on the soccer team, and in athletics . . ." He chewed at his thumbnail. "It isn't fair." He looked at her sideways. "Couldn't you make it go away? I mean, if I never went to court, then maybe it'd be okay with the school, like it never happened."

"It did happen, David, and I've already told your father I'm not going to try to pull any strings for you."

Sliding farther down in the seat, he repeated, "It isn't fair."

"Not fair?" Carol could hear her voice rising. "What isn't fair is that you went ahead without any thought of the consequences, not only for you, but for other people. I don't mean just your father and me, but what about the kids you supplied and their families? Have you thought about that?"

He bit his lip. She could see tears in his eyes, so she said, "David, it isn't the end of the world, but you're in for some unpleasant times ahead."

He hunched his shoulders and turned his face

away from her. They didn't speak for the rest of the trip.

Sybil's house was set up high, with a beguiling view of sky, ocean and sand. The crescent of the beach was bracketed by tall sandstone cliffs, so weathered by time that their profiles brooded like ancient faces contemplating the sea that pounded the rock platforms at their bases.

David was out of the car almost before Carol stopped in the sloping driveway. "Sybil? I'm here!"

Carol caught a flash of her red hair, then Sybil was down the steps and hugging him. David had first met Sybil Quade when he was nine and she and Carol had started living together. He loved her with an uncomplicated pleasure. She took him swimming and fishing and never criticized him. In short, Carol thought, Sybil was the perfect aunt, which was good, because he had no real aunts, as both Carol and Justin had been only children.

Carol went to get out of the car, but Sybil put a hand up to stop her. "Carol, I know you've got a lot to do, so just go. All I need to know is when you want David home."

"Is five too late?"

"Not at all. He'll be there."

Carol watched them walk up the steep steps to the front door, very conscious that Sybil didn't want to have a conversation with her. Didn't want her in the house. At the top of the steps the two of them turned to wave as Carol began to back down the drive. Sybil had put on a little weight since they had first met, and it suited her.

Felicity Banning had agreed to meet Carol and Bourke at eleven. Carol checked her watch, finding she had plenty of time, so she took the longer route along the shoreline. The coast north of the central city had beautiful beach after beautiful beach, and she found herself soothed by the brilliance of the blue water and the roll of the whitecaps. Heavy winds had created a high swell, so Carol took a back road at Mona Vale Hospital and parked for a few minutes on a miniature headland to view the surf crashing onto the barrier of the land. It was exciting and calming at the same time. She wound down the window and let the wind strike her face with exhilarating force. The thump of the waves seemed to vibrate through the rock, and fine salt mist flung into the air by the shattering breakers peppered the windscreen of her car. She could taste the astringency on her lips.

As she started the car and wound up her window, she had a sudden thought. The window in Banning's Rolls-Royce had been open, but why? It had been cold and showery that morning, and she thought it unlikely that a man like him, accustomed to luxury, would set off with wet wintry air blowing in on him.

When she got to the Banning house, Mark Bourke was waiting for her. "I almost made it. Two minutes late at the most," she said.

"I got here a bit ahead of time."

They grinned at each other. Carol always cut it fine: Bourke was always early.

Carol surveyed the Bannings's home. The double garage, with dark brown doors shut, was under the front of the house. Steps led up from the side of the driveway to the entrance door. There was no garden in the front, and the house itself was generic red brick with cream trim.

Felicity Banning opened the front door before they reached the top of the sandstone steps. "Inspector Ashton," she said, her voice toneless. She nodded politely to Bourke. "Would you please come in."

Carol glanced around as they were led down a hallway and into a light-filled room at the end. Banning had been extremely rich, but money clearly didn't buy taste. The furniture was obviously costly, but nothing matched. A heavy brass-based coffee table with a glass top sat between two bulbous lounges upholstered with an eye-assaulting floral pattern. A cane magazine holder was crammed with newspapers and periodicals. The floor was polished wood, with scatter rugs of various hues. The assertive red-and-cream striped pattern of the wallpaper was largely hidden by crowding paintings and photographs, the frames of which ranged from ornate gold to minimalist thin black. A Swedish-style blond wooden desk had a fat magenta chair behind it.

"Please sit down," said Felicity Banning, indicating one of the lounges. She sank into its portly twin and folded her hands on her lap. For all its plumpness, Carol found the lounge uncomfortable, so she sat forward, not wanting to settle into its fat depths. "Thank you for seeing us."

Felicity Banning nodded wearily. "Would you like coffee, tea?" When they both declined, she went on, "I can still hardly believe that Walter's dead. I expect him to walk through the door any moment, and say it was all a dreadful mistake."

In contrast to Cardover's acerbic wife, who had shown no signs of grief, this woman was obviously suffering. Her face was pale, there were purple-black circles under her eyes, and she looked as if she'd recently been weeping. She was, Carol estimated, about forty-five, and dressed in dowdy but high-priced clothes. She'd pinned up her hair with tortoiseshell combs, but strands of light brown hair were escaping to hang over her face.

Carol said, "I've read the statement you gave to Detective Sergeant Bourke, and it was very comprehensive, but there are a few more questions."

Absently rubbing the crease between her eyebrows with a knuckle, she said, "I've already said I can't imagine anyone who would want to kill Walter."

"You're aware that his partner, Eric Cardover, died on Friday morning?"

"Yes. I called Phyllis to offer my condolences." She gave a tired half-smile. "Which was more than she did for me."

Carol couldn't think of a way to be gentle with her next question, so she said baldly, "We're wondering if there might be some connection between the two deaths."

Surprise broke through the misery on Felicity Banning's face. "There's something suspicious about Eric's death? I thought he had another stroke."

"We don't know yet," said Bourke, "but there is some possibility that Mr. Cardover didn't die of natural causes."

She seemed grateful to have something puzzling to consider. "Eric murdered? Would that mean it might be something to do with Banning and Cardover? We didn't see each other socially, so we had no friends in common, or, for that matter, enemies. The business was the only link."

"What happens to the company now?"

"It's split between the families, but Walter had fifty-five percent and Eric forty-five. I suppose the controlling interest is mine, as we had no children." She sighed. "Not that I give a damn at the moment. I've no idea who'll run the business." With a faint smile she added, "Of course, Jonathan Cardover has ambitions to be the top dog. Phyllis has already suggested it."

Bourke said, "When we had our first interview, I asked you if you'd think about any specific individuals who might want to harm your husband. Now I'd like you to consider if there are people with a serious grudge against *both* men."

Without hesitation, she said, "Environmentalists. The company has been the target of protests over many projects, but the mining in New Guinea triggered the worst of them. Both Walter and Eric received a barrage of intimidating messages promising physical harm, and worse. I recall that Walter said that Eric was so incensed he was considering legal action."

"Do you have any details? Names?"

Felicity Banning shook her head at Bourke's question. "Walter's assistant may know."

"Did they take any steps to protect themselves?"

She shrugged. "You have to realize that this is par for the course. Every development, every mine, gets its share of protesters, and many of them are menacing. There's been some violence with demonstrations at different sites, but never any attempt at a physical attack on my husband or Cardover. There was no reason to think things were different this time."

Carol said, "I need to ask you something about finding your husband's body."

Felicity Banning visibly braced herself. "Yes?"

"When you went down to the garage, the car engine was idling and the passenger window was wound down. Is that right? You didn't open it yourself?"

She swallowed. "No. I remember I put my hands on the sill when I saw the blood. It was bizarre, like a movie, and I couldn't believe what had happened. I didn't scream. I touched him, I saw his face, and I knew he was dead." She stared ahead, as though seeing it all replaying on a screen. "Just a few minutes before we were talking in the kitchen."

Carol glanced at Bourke to indicate she wasn't going to pursue this area. He nodded toward the pale wooden desk. "I wonder if you've got around to checking through your husband's papers?"

"I'm sorry, Sergeant, I haven't had time." She lifted her hands, then dropped them back into her lap. "That's a lie, actually. I've had the time, but I just can't seem to do anything."

Carol could imagine the numb desolation she must be feeling. "Your husband's body will be released tomorrow, so you're free to make funeral arrangements."

"Funeral arrangements?" she said blankly. "Yes, of course." She seemed to shrink, as though this additional demand was more than she could cope with.

"Do you have someone who could help?" asked Carol.

"My sister." She rallied to add, "Thank you for your concern, Inspector. I'll be okay."

They asked a few more questions, but it was clear to Carol that it would be better to wait until Banning's widow had got over her initial shock.

When she and Bourke were outside in the street, he said, "If she murdered her husband, she's the world's greatest actor."

Carol was inclined to agree, but she said, "There is always that possibility. We've both seen Academy Award performances in our time."

"These vague environmentalists making threats — we need names."

"Just the job for you, Mark," said Carol.

"I'll ask Anne to do it. She's into that sort of thing."

Carol raised an eyebrow. Anne Newsome had never struck her as the type to belong to any protest group. "Tell her to concentrate on the New Guinea operation. That seems to have got the most attention."

Before they went to their cars, Bourke said, "Don't forget tomorrow night." His mouth quirked. "You can't get out of it. I heard you promise Pat. Besides, there's a bonus. The premier will be there."

"Well, that's a real plus," she said sardonically.

"There's more," said Bourke. "Free wine and cheese. And high quality hors d'oeuvres."

"Tempting."

"I guarantee the quality of the food. Pat may be on maternity leave from the gallery, but she can't resist organizing everything. Besides, you like Aboriginal art."

Pat was prominent in the Sydney art world and had recently struck out on her own with a gallery featuring young and up-and-coming artists. At first it had seemed strange to think of the pragmatic Bourke marrying someone in that field; however, their marriage was clearly a success. In all the years she'd worked with him, Carol had never seen Bourke so happy. And the birth of his daughter had been the icing on the cake. As he'd said to her, grinning to protect himself from seeming too intense, his life was complete.

After telling Bourke to assure Pat she'd be there no matter what, Carol got into her car. She was intending to go to the office to review the papers on the Fader case, but instead she found herself driving to Long Bay Jail where Matthew Bott was being held. There was no real reason for her to see him herself, but in some way she felt she owed it to Nicola Bratt. She couldn't imagine why this particular case had become important to her; the assault and occasional murder of transients was a fact of life in a large metropolis like Sydney. Maybe it was the care with which the woman had kept her papers and driver's license. Perhaps once she had owned a car and had driven the streets like any ordinary citizen.

Traffic was light, and she was soon parking her car in a lot crowded with the vehicles of people spending Sunday afternoon visiting friends and relatives in jail. Carol was accustomed to the smells and sounds of incarceration, but she could never get to the point of ignoring them. She had sent so many criminals to soulless places like this, secure in the belief that they deserved their punishment, but she knew that she would hardly be able to endure being caged, institutionalized.

She was only in the grimy interview room for a

few moments before Bott was led in. He was a slight, inoffensive figure with gray face, thin hair and shaking hands. He bobbed his head respectfully at her then slid onto the wooden seat on the other side of the table.

"You killed Nicola Bratt," she said.

He looked past her at the wall. "Yeah," he agreed. "I did."

"Why?"

Wriggling his narrow shoulders, he said querulously, "Her fault. She wouldn't give me what was mine." A spark of enthusiasm lit his face. "You got a fag?"

"No."

He subsided, bending his neck so she couldn't see his rheumy eyes. Carol said, "Did you know her personally?"

"Nic? Yeah. She'd been around for years. Sure you haven't got a fag?"

"I don't smoke."

He grunted, discontented, then began to scratch the back of one spotted hand.

Carol shook her head. What answers had she hoped to find? Feeling faintly ridiculous to be there at all, she signaled for the guard.

CHAPTER SIX

Monday morning Carol and David left early so that she could swing by Justin's eastern suburbs home and drop him off. Glancing over at her son when they were stopped at traffic lights, she wondered again what Sybil had said to him. He'd come back yesterday afternoon pensive and unusually silent. When she'd asked, David has said in a vague way, "We talked about things." Then, after a pause, he'd said, "Mum, I'm sorry about what happened. It was a really dumb thing to do."

She'd given him a tight hug. "We'll work things out."

When she parked in front of Justin's palatial home, a building of well-mannered extravagance, she went in with David to have a quick talk with Justin and Eleanor, but her ex-husband had already left for chambers. While David clattered upstairs to unpack his bag, Carol succumbed to the smell of freshly brewed coffee. It took little urging for Eleanor to get Carol to sit at the kitchen table with a steaming mug in front of her.

"This is heaven," she said after her first sip. "At work I drink something black that claims to be coffee, but it's closer to a combination of liquid tar with a jolt of caffeine."

They chatted about inconsequential things for a few moments, then Eleanor said, "Did you get through to David? Justin just yells, or is coldly furious, neither of which seems to be working."

"I did some yelling of my own," said Carol with a rueful smile. "Actually, the person who seems to have made a difference is Sybil. David spent some time with her at the beach yesterday, and he came back a lot less combative and considerably more thoughtful."

"You and Sybil — " Eleanor let her voice trail off, her expression politely hopeful.

"I'm afraid not."

Eleanor looked a little embarrassed. "I'm sorry. I shouldn't have mentioned it."

"It's okay," said Carol, thinking that it wasn't really okay at all. She suddenly realized that she was furious with Sybil because yesterday she'd left David at Carol's front gate and had refused to come down to see the alterations to the house.

"The media have got hold of the story," said Eleanor. "Did you see the paper this morning?"

"I've got it in the car to glance at if I have a moment at work, but I didn't have time to even look at the headlines before we left this morning."

Eleanor passed over the newspaper. "Third page, top left corner. Justin has already been pestered by reporters."

It was exactly what Carol had expected. No names could be given out, of course, as the students were legally children, but all it took was a quick phone call from a cop or a teacher, and the families involved would be common knowledge. Carol was sure there'd be messages waiting for her at work. Journalists would be delighted to find that one of the kids suspended had not one, but *two* high-profile parents.

School Suspends Five for Use of Cannabis

Students at an exclusive North Shore private school have been suspended for allegedly possessing and smoking cannabis. The headmaster issued a statement saying that the school had a tough stance on drugs, and that if the charges were substantiated, the students would be expelled.

"The trouble is," said Eleanor, "that this must be the third or fourth case in private schools where kids have been caught with marijuana in the last few months. I imagine David and the others will be used as sobering object lessons, to show what will happen if rules get broken."

David crashed down the stairs and bounced into the kitchen. "I'm starving. What's to eat?"

"I fed you breakfast," Carol protested.

"Mum, that was hours ago."

He seemed to have recovered his good spirits, flinging open the refrigerator and examining the contents in search of a food fix. Carol interrupted him to kiss him good-bye, well aware that he would wriggle in her embrace and turn his cheek away. "You're such a fake," she said. "You know you just love to be cuddled." David gave her a macho look and went back to the fridge.

Eleanor walked Carol out to her car. "Do you think he realizes how serious this is?" she asked Carol.

"He's starting to. David's full of bravado on the surface, but I know he's quite devastated at the prospect of leaving school and his friends there."

"His father is pulling strings, but it may not be all that easy to get David enrolled in a suitable place, or at least one acceptable to Justin."

Carol grinned. "I suggested the local public high school, but Justin wasn't keen."

"I can imagine," said Eleanor, amused.

Approaching police headquarters from a new direction was no help with the traffic, which was just as heavy as the route Carol usually took from the North

Shore. Normally impatient, this morning it didn't worry her that she was constantly stopping and starting, only to crawl along at what seemed walking speed, as she used the time to review her active cases. Matthew Bott would be arraigned for murder today. The trial, when it eventually came up in the docket, would be a foregone conclusion, and Bott would probably spend the rest of his life behind bars.

As far as the Fader case was concerned, the DNA test results were due today, and if they implicated the brother, as expected, then he would be arrested and charged.

Walter Banning's murder was another matter altogether. Banning & Cardover was the privately held controlling company of a conglomerate of public companies. It was likely that the demise of both principals would have serious implications for the share prices of those other companies. Cardover's death might still be a natural one, but Banning had been deliberately killed, and the motive for his murder could lie in his business dealings or in his private relationships.

Why this victim? And why now? It fascinated Carol — the unraveling of another's life to search for patterns. In day-to-day living, no one ever saw the complexity that made up an individual, but only the particular aspects that he or she revealed to a spouse or a friend or a business colleague. In the detailed investigation of a violent death, however, those many aspects were compared and contrasted, and although at times Carol had been baffled by the enigma that was the victim, the hidden central self of the person was often exposed.

As soon as she arrived, Bourke handed her a

folder. "Postmortem on Banning, and nothing new. And ballistics can't match the slugs. They're twenty-twos, that's all they'll say."

"Not much help."

"I've got Banning's personal assistant, Valerie Rule, coming in this morning. Do you want to see her?"

"We'll interview her together."

"One bit of positive news," said Bourke. "We've got a positive match for the blood DNA at the crime scene and Fader's brother."

Carol felt the relief of a case being wound up. "With the other evidence, that's enough. Arrest him."

Bourke shook his head. "Just a stupid fight that got out of hand," he said.

The murder had been both senseless and unnecessary. A simple argument between the two Fader brothers about how to run their repair shop had escalated into bloody combat, ending with one lying on the greasy floor with his head beaten in. The other had had the presence of mind to shower in the washroom that was attached to the workshop, change clothes, then "discover" his brother's body. He'd explained his own bruised face and broken nose as resulting from a fall, but DNA samples of blood at the scene had now irrevocably tied him to the crime.

Carol wondered what seeds of bitter resentment and anger lay in the past between the brothers, only needing the flashpoint of this trivial conflict to burst into deadly action.

Bourke followed Carol as she headed for her office. "No interesting fingerprints in the Cardover room at the hospital, but I'm keeping it sealed until the postmortem."

"Dr. Olson isn't pleased, I imagine."

"Not pleased at all. He's already called the super and complained."

As Carol dumped her briefcase on her desk and began taking papers out of it, Bourke said, "And one more thing. Anne's got a bee in her bonnet about some way-out Web site she found on the Internet while she was researching groups on record as protesting against Banning's companies. She says she's got at least one suspicious death that could be linked to Banning's."

Carol stopped. "One of his colleagues?"

"No, some guy out shooting kangaroos west of Dubbo in the middle of nowhere. Guthrie was his name. She got the Dubbo cops to fax the information this morning." He pointed to her in-box. "There it is."

Carol raised her eyebrows at her young detective constable. "So, Anne, Edward Guthrie gets killed by a stray shot while he's spotlighting kangaroos. That's one for the 'roos, but I've read the report on his death, and that's all I can see."

"It may not have been an accident."

Carol's elderly desk chair creaked as she leaned back in it. The pseudo-leather was cracking, and the swiveling mechanism had started making ominous grinding noises. She wasn't relishing the bureaucratic effort that requisitioning a new one would require, but it seemed inevitable in the near future.

Anne Newsome, zealous, was waiting for her response. Carol said, "There were other shooters out there racing around in the dark, weren't there? I'd say a fair number of them would blaze away at anything that moves. Why not a shot that went astray from some idiot who fancies himself a hunter?" She shoved the report across the desk. "Have another look, Anne. The coroner's going to come in with a verdict of accidental death. Shooting by person or persons unknown. Hunters get killed every year by other hunters."

"It looks to me like there was a contract out on Guthrie."

Carol repressed a smile at Anne's confident assertion. She reminded Carol of herself at Anne's age. "And just how do you know that?"

"There's a list of names on a Web site called Gaia's Revenge. It's an environmental group headquartered in the States, but it's got branches all over the world. Anyway, Edward Guthrie's name is on the site, and so is Walter Banning's. I've printed out the relevant stuff." As she handed Carol a green plastic folder, she said, "You know about Gaia?"

"Vaguely. I have the impression it's New-Ageish. The earth's a living organism, or something like that, isn't it?"

"It's explained in a preamble on the Web site. In Greek myth Gaia is the goddess of the whole earth. Now the word *Gaia* applies to the idea that all the interdependent systems of life operate together, like some immense personality. Gaia is supposed to be self-correcting, so when anything seriously threatens the earth, it has to be changed, or, if that doesn't work, destroyed."

"So that would mean humans would be one of Gaia's main problems?" said Carol, her tone flippant.

Anne didn't smile. "Exactly," she said.

Carol opened the folder and surveyed the tidily arranged contents. "I didn't realize you'd been infected by Mark's desire for order." Glancing at the papers covering her desk, she added, "I'm obviously immune."

Anne's expression remained neutral, and wisely, Carol thought, the constable made no comment.

"Mark tells me you belong to a protest group. Is it something like Gaia?"

Ann reddened slightly. "I'm on the board of an animal rights' organization, Creatures' Comfort." She gave Carol a semi defiant look. "Not radical, really." She gestured toward the open folder. "I didn't realize it before, but our organization, along with a lot of others, is linked to the Gaia's Revenge Web site. I've printed a list of them."

Carol turned pages until she found the typed column of names. There were about fifteen, organizations around the world that were concerned about the destruction of tropical rain forests, the degradation of wild animals' habitats, the spoliation of the sea, the rights of animals, and the marketing of genetically engineered foods. "These include extremist groups."

Anne said, "Certainly some of them are fanatics, like the bunch who were involved in kidnaping that Oxford biochemist last year, or the group who claimed responsibility for sinking the Japanese whaling vessel."

"And what's the connection between Gaia and Banning?"

"Look at the final page."

NOTABLE DELETIONS was the heading. The months from January to December were listed for the current year, and under each one were names in alphabetical order, each with a location and comment. Under August, Carol read:

> BANNING, WALTER. Sydney, New South Wales, Australia. Defiler of streams. Polluter. Exploiter of labor. Corrupter of officials.
> GUTHRIE, EDWARD. Near Dubbo, New South Wales, Australia. Environmental vandal.

"Why is Edward Guthrie an environmental vandal?" Carol asked.

"He's got a huge tourist development on an island off the Queensland coast that's supposed to have put so much pollution into the water that the coral reefs nearby are dying."

Carol scanned the rest of the names. One caught her attention. "I see Herman Ratner is here under June," she said. "He certainly died from natural causes, not assassination. Had a heart attack in front of a dining room of supporters in Tokyo."

The death of Ratner had been front-page news two months before. The British mining magnate, who had had a succession of scandalous divorces, had been a larger-than-life character who had built a fortune with dubious mining deals, many in Third World countries. He'd been at a banquet to announce his latest venture when he'd suffered a fatal heart seizure.

Carol looked up to find Anne looking at her intently. Carol said, "It might be macabre to catalog names this way, Anne, but not against the law. When something happens to an individual Gaia's Revenge considers a polluter, or worse, the name is added to the list. Now, if the name of a victim was added *before* his or her death, *that* would be suspicious."

"Look at the locations under each month," said Anne. "There's something interesting."

Carol studied the page for a moment. "I see what you mean. The deaths are clustered in geographical areas."

Three were listed for the United States over the January–February period, and a fourth death in Canada. March had two in Britain and one in Belgium. April was blank, then May detailed two in Brazil. June had Ratner in Tokyo and someone with a Japanese name in Kyoto. July didn't follow the rule: The four locations were South Africa, Ireland, Indonesia and Italy. Carol frowned over the last name for that month. "Martina Isadora sounds vaguely familiar."

"I know all about her because of Creatures' Comfort," said Anne with loathing. "She ran mink farms and supplied most of the high-fashion designers in Europe." Her jaw tightened. "She was no loss." Her color rose. "I'm sorry, I shouldn't have said that, but the conditions for the animals were horrific, as was the way they were killed."

"Okay, so this list has some despicable people on it. So where do we go from there?"

"I think it's a hit list." Anne looked pugnacious. "I know it sounds far-fetched, but it could be true."

"Anne, that's way over the top. Members of this Gaia organization have an inventory of people they're delighted have died, because now they can't do any more damage."

Anne tilted her head. "You're probably right, but can I check it out further?"

Handing back the green folder, Carol said, "Okay, it's a long shot, but see what you can find out. I'd be interested to know if Gaia's Revenge has an Australian branch."

"They do," said Anne, getting up. "I'll get the details for you."

Gaia's Revenge, thought Carol, shaking her head at the name. No doubt they were well-meaning environmentalists who made a pointed comment by cataloging the deaths of those they considered enemies of the earth. She sat back, her chair creaking arthritically. It was highly unlikely scenario, but what if they were a terrorist group? What if there was a team of global serial killers, and it was Australia's turn to play host?

CHAPTER SEVEN

"Frankly, Inspector Ashton, I'm surprised you didn't ask to see me earlier. I've been Walter Banning's personal assistant for over twenty-five years. I know everything about him."

Valerie Rule had, Carol thought, an interesting/ugly face. She had a pug nose, a heavy jaw, and bulbous blue eyes, but the overall impression was somehow quite acceptable. She wore an undeniably expensive cashmere suit and a double string of pearls.

"You saw all of Mr. Banning's correspondence?" asked Bourke.

"All of it. Personal and business. Nothing went across his desk I didn't see."

"Did he receive any threats in the last few months?"

Valerie Rule made a derisive sound. "Really, Sergeant Bourke," she said in the tone of one speaking to someone not very bright, "a man in Mr. Banning's position received threats of one type or another almost every week. Of course, he rarely saw them. Part of my duties was to screen him from irrelevant or annoying communications, however they were delivered."

With a look of satisfaction she added, "No one, and I mean *no one*, had access to Walter Banning unless I said so." She reached for the attaché case beside her chair. "I've brought the file containing letters that I kept because I deemed them serious enough to hold for future reference." She took out a red folder and handed it to Carol. "Perhaps you'd care to check these out."

"Is there any pattern that you've noticed?"

"Oh, yes. Apart from the mentally disturbed, there're plenty of those tree-huggers. Loony conservationists who protest against any development just as a matter of course."

"Any particular group?"

Displeased, she sighed. "Inspector, I'm far too busy to remember the name of every little radical organization. They'll be in the file."

Bourke asked, "Did Mr. Banning ever meet with representatives of any of these environmental groups?"

"Of course not," she snorted. "And I wouldn't have allowed it, anyway. His time was far too valuable to spend with individuals whose main idea is to stand in the way of progress." She flicked one hand in a dismissive gesture. "They make a lot of noise, but that sort of person doesn't have the guts to *do* anything. I believe you should look elsewhere."

Thinking with a trace of amusement that Valerie Rule was under the impression she was running the interview, Carol said, "Can you think of anyone who would be capable of murdering Mr. Banning?"

"Plenty who'd want him dead, but again, not many with the guts to do it." Her pug nose twitched. "Of course, there's always Jonathan Cardover. I imagine he's your main suspect."

"Indeed?"

She gave Carol a quick, affirmative nod. "Thinks he knows it all, and couldn't wait to get some power in the company. The moment Mr. Cardover had his stroke, Jonathan was going through his desk. He fired Marcie Evans quick smart, and moved into his father's office." Her lips tightened in distaste. "Jonathan installed his own assistant. Rexie her name is. Anorexic and skirts short enough to show her crotch."

Carol saw Bourke repress a smile. He checked his notes and said, "Marcie Evans had the equivalent of your position with Mr. Cardover?"

"I wouldn't say she had quite the close professional relationship that I enjoyed with Mr. Banning, but Marcie had been with the company almost fifteen years. Of course, she never had much time for Jonathan, and he knew it. Not half the talent of his father, but ambition enough for ten."

"You said you believed Jonathan Cardover would be our main suspect. Why is that?" Carol asked.

Valerie Rule smiled grimly. "Perhaps you haven't been told about the altercation he had with Mr. Banning two days before the murder."

"A heated argument?"

"I should say so." She seemed gratified to be providing the information. "I could hear it through the closed door. Mr. Banning never suffered fools gladly, and he didn't have a high opinion of Jonathan Cardover. Jonathan yelled something about how it was time for new blood at the top of the company, and Mr. Banning told him what he thought of that."

With a small smile, Bourke said, "He wasn't in favor?"

She pursed her lips. "Mr. Banning said, very emphatically, that Jonathan would get any influence about company policy over his dead body. Those were his exact words. A moment later Jonathan stormed out, slamming the door behind him." She paused to let this sink in, then added, "No breeding, like his mother."

"I've met Felicity Cardover," said Carol.

"Yes," said Valerie Rule. Apparently she trusted that Carol's impressions of Cardover's widow had been in line with hers.

"It's just a formality, but where were you the morning Mr. Banning died?" asked Bourke.

His question amused Valerie Rule. "I don't think you'll find I'm a viable suspect, Sergeant Bourke. I was already in the office. I always get in very early, around seven, and several people can vouch for me. Before that, I was home with my husband. No doubt Donald will confirm that."

After a few more questions about Banning's schedule for the week he died, Bourke showed Valerie Rule out. Coming back to Carol's office, he announced, "I can tell you, I wouldn't like to be Donald Rule!"

Grinning, Carol said, "Check out everything she

said, Mark. There's one woman I don't doubt is capable of murder if the fancy took her."

Late in the afternoon Anne came into Carol's office with a triumphant smile. "I've located the local Gaia's Revenge branch. It's in Glebe. And I've spoken to the guy who runs it, Gerald Fitch. He can see us first thing tomorrow."

"I've got an appointment at ten," said Carol, thinking of Loren Reece.

"Fitch said he'd be there from eight o'clock on."

"Okay, we'll go together. And run a check on him, Anne. I want to know if he has a record."

"There's another thing," said Anne. "I logged on to the Gaia site, and Eric Cardover's name has been added to the list."

The art exhibition at Pat's gallery started at six. Carol had brought a change of clothes, so she grabbed a quick shower at work and arrived only a few minutes after the hour with the pleasant feeling that she was looking her best in a pale green dress that had been outrageously expensive and looked it.

The gallery was in Paddington, so it was only a short distance to drive. Finding a parking spot was a challenge, but she was lucky on her third trip around the block of terrace houses, snapping up a space when someone obligingly pulled out.

Quite a few people had already arrived, and Carol greeted several she knew. Waiters were circulating with wine and trays of hors d'oeuvres, and Carol noted that Bourke's undertaking that the food would be excellent was fulfilled. Glass in one hand and tiny spinach pastry in the other, she looked around for Pat. She saw with surprise that Sam Goolwa was standing on the other side of the room, deep in conversation with a striking Aboriginal woman.

When Carol made her way over to them, Goolwa beamed at her. "Inspector, I didn't know you'd be here. Let me introduce you to one of the artists, Yvonne Gardinal. Yvonne, this is Inspector Ashton."

Carol was interested to see how much more self-assurance Goolwa had out of work. She shook hands with the young woman, who seemed hardly more than a teenager. "Is this one of yours?" Carol asked, indicating a canvas glowing with a pattern of rich ocher and red earth colors.

"Yes, it is," she answered, her voice almost a whisper. "And those two next to it."

They were striking works, confidently executed. Carol was delighted to give sincere praise rather than polite compliments. Someone arrived to sweep Yvonne and Goolwa away to meet the premier, who had just arrived, leaving Carol to contemplate the paintings alone. She felt a touch on her shoulder.

"Carol," said Pat, "you kept your promise. Now, tell me it was worth it. Some spectacular stuff, don't you agree?"

"It is." She smiled at Bourke's wife. Pat was tall, rather angular, and had a plain, pleasant face. "How's Carli?"

"You've had enough talk about the baby from Mark, I'm sure," said Pat, "so I'll spare you any more. Suffice it to say she's gorgeous. When I left home,

Mark and Carli were cooing at each other, and it would be hard to say who was having the most fun."

Pat took Carol's arm. "There's someone who's asked to meet you. Come with me."

Pat strode through the room with assurance, Carol following in her wake. It had become appreciably more crowded, and Pat greeted people by name as she passed them. Some seemed to be actively admiring the artworks, but judging from the hum of conversation, with a greeting or a loud laugh rising above the blur of words, quite a number were treating this strictly as a social occasion. A tight cluster had gravitated toward the premier and his wife, as if, Carol thought wryly, they could gain something tangible by proximity to the chief politician in the state.

Pat halted in front of a woman in sleek black, who stood alone studying a canvas. "As required, I'm delivering Carol Ashton," said Pat. Carol, this is Loren Reece."

"We're meeting a little earlier than expected," said the woman, extending her hand.

Her grasp was firm and quick. She was about Carol's height, but slightly heavier, and she had the broad shoulders Carol always associated with competitive swimming.

"Loren has just bought two paintings," said Pat, "so when she said she'd like to meet you, Carol, I said if that's what you want, you've got it."

When Pat was claimed by an acquaintance and excused herself, Carol said, "You collect art?"

"Not really. They're gifts for friends. I'm not into art investment."

Carol assessed her. Mid-thirties maybe, and with the healthy glow of someone secure in an active body.

She had deep brown hair, beautifully styled, direct dark eyes, and an amused curve to her mouth.

"Do I pass muster?" she asked.

Carol felt a faint embarrassment. "Sorry, it's an occupational hazard." To change the subject, she said, "I believe you know the premier."

"Yes, I interviewed him last year when I was doing a travel series on the South Pacific. It was by chance, but my article about Australia appeared in the States about the same time that the New South Wales Tourism Board launched an advertising campaign there." She grinned. "That means I'm in favor, at least at the moment."

She disliked making small talk, but Carol found herself saying, "You travel a lot in your job, I imagine."

"Constantly. Just in the last months I've been in Russia, China and Thailand gathering information for the articles on female law enforcement officers for which I'm contracted." She gave Carol a charming smile. "Of course, that's why I asked to interview you."

"I have very little time at the moment," said Carol, intending to dampen the journalist's enthusiasm.

"Walter Banning's murder."

When Carol looked at her with surprise, Loren went on, "I research all my subjects thoroughly."

"I can see that."

Loren laughed at Carol's resigned tone. "I guarantee," she said, "that the process will be painless. In fact, you'll enjoy it."

"Loren?" The premier's wife beckoned.

"Not a summons I can ignore," said Loren. "I'll see you tomorrow."

Carol watched her move away. Even in high heels she had the stride of an athlete. As though she knew Carol was watching, Loren turned her head and gave her a quizzical smile. Carol's previous irritation about the journalist's demand to see her evaporated. This was an interesting, self-assured woman, and Carol looked forward to seeing her again.

CHAPTER EIGHT

The little, inner-city office building was on a side street off Glebe Point Road, set incongruously with small private houses. There were two stories, and the brickwork was painted a pale yellow, with brown trim at the windows and doors. The lower floor held a therapy practice, its presence indicated by a large sign that declared emphatically, THERAPY, SINGLES AND COUPLES, HERE!

A woman, face buried in a large white handkerchief, came out the central door and blundered into

Carol and Anne. "Sorry," she said indistinctly, before hurrying away.

Anne made a face at Carol. "Looks to me like the therapy isn't working."

Carol, remembering her own experiences when she'd been forced to go to a police psychologist after being wounded on duty, didn't comment. It hadn't been a pleasant experience, but she'd reluctantly admitted to herself that psychotherapy might sometimes be of help. She rarely cried, but she recalled how those sessions had loosened her natural reserve to the point of tears.

GAIA'S REVENGE was written under an arrow that pointed up a narrow flight of stairs that ran up the side of the building. The door at the top had an opaque glass panel with attached hand-lettered sign that instructed visitors to ring the bell.

Carol obediently pressed the button, and a two-tone chime sounded inside. After a moment they heard the sound of a lock being turned, and the door was opened by a middle-aged man in a wrinkled blue suit.

"Come in," he said. "Sorry about the locked door, but we have to keep the ratbags out, you know."

He led them into a small room furnished with white cane sofa and chairs and so full of ferns and other greenery that it seemed like a conservatory. The walls were covered with posters exhorting the saving of the natural world. One warned in stark red letters: GAIA WILL HAVE HER REVENGE.

He turned to shake hands with Carol, and then with Anne. "Gerald Fitch at your service," he said. "Do make yourselves comfortable. Herb tea?"

"Thank you, no," said Carol. She hated herb tea

with a passion, lumping the beverage in with all flavored or scented drinks.

He smiled, as though reading her mind. "I'm sorry. We don't have coffee."

Fitch took a cane chair opposite them, leaning forward so his hands dangled between his knees. He didn't look at all like the stereotypical rabid conservationist that Carol couldn't help holding in her mind. He had no facial hair, no ponytail, no crumpled cotton shirt or thick sandals. In fact, he looked like an inoffensive small businessman, struggling to make ends meet. His shirt was roughly ironed, his tie knotted so one end was much longer than the other, his black shoes needed a polish, and he'd nicked his chin shaving.

Anne took out her notebook. Fitch grinned. "Ah, an official interview. I've had a lot of those."

Carol knew that was true. Gerald Fitch had been arrested many times. He had paddled out to nuclear submarines, he had chained himself to logging machinery, he had lain down in front of a motorcade for a visiting head of state, he had picketed the head offices of mining companies.

"Walter Banning and Eric Cardover have both recently died," Carol said. "We're interested to see their names appear on your Web site."

"It's not my Web site," he said. "It belongs to our worldwide movement. On it you will see the names of defilers, contaminators, destroyers of our planet." His mild face was suddenly suffused with anger. "Do you have any idea what Cardover and Banning have done? They put their bloody companies in undeveloped countries where there are few, if any, environmental controls, and they despoil the rivers, make the air foul with fumes and dust, destroy the habitat of countless creatures."

Fitch looked from Carol to Anne. "Have you ever seen the children affected by this? I have." He shook his head. "The pity of it. Kids whose health and happiness have been destroyed. And why? For greed. These are vile men who corrupted everything they touched. I'm delighted that they're both dead." He glowered at them, seeming to dare them to make a comment.

Carol said, "Mr. Banning was murdered. Is it possible that one of your followers could have been involved?"

He sat back to consider her question. "It's not impossible. Those who love Gaia are well aware that criminals like Banning and his cronies should be eliminated for the good of us all. As far as actually killing the man, if I could name someone, I wouldn't." His smile was grim as he added, "I would congratulate the person privately for carrying out a necessary execution."

"Would you provide us with a list of your members?"

"I suppose you'll get a court order if I don't?"

"You suppose right," said Carol.

He rubbed his chin. "It'll take a few days. I've got to admit I'm a bit behind as far as getting things organized."

"As soon as possible, please." After getting his reluctant nod, she went on. "Have you or anyone in Gaia's Revenge ever communicated directly with Banning or Cardover?"

Fitch's expression made it clear he considered this a pointless question. "Well, of course we have, Inspector. Every time they started a new project to destroy the integrity of an environment somewhere in the world we protested, along with many other concerned groups."

Carol looked over at Anne, who said to Fitch, "Have you actually met either Mr. Banning or Mr. Cardover?"

"Banning I have. Fronted him in his offices in Pitt Street. Bluffed my way past the dragon of a woman who guards him and spoke to him face to face." With a look of disgust he said, "He cowered behind his big desk and screamed for security. I made my point and then walked out."

"The names on your site look like a hit list," said Anne.

"A hit list?" Fitch said, amused. "That wasn't the intention. So far we merely record each name when we learn that a notable enemy of Gaia has been eliminated, by whatever means." He looked at Anne with approval. "Actually, you make a good point, Constable. I'll recommend that we consider a listing of those eco-criminals whose crimes make them worthy of assassination. Then you could call it an invitation to murder, if you like."

Carol said, "Is the name Edward Guthrie familiar to you?"

"Guthrie? He ruined pristine rain forest and the runoff from his bloody resort killed coral reefs in the area. I was happy when I heard of his unfortunate accident while he was slaughtering kangaroos."

Fitch's mouth twisted with disgust. "Guthrie was one of those moral cripples who make themselves feel like big men by killing things. It was poetic justice that some other subhuman blazing away in the dark shot him."

"You seem to know a lot about the incident," Carol observed.

He gave her a wolfish smile. "Think I went to the outback and put a bullet in his throat, Inspector? It wasn't me, but I'd have been proud to have done it."

When Carol asked for Fitch's whereabouts on Thursday morning at the time when Banning was murdered, he replied that he lived alone and came into the office early every weekday morning. "If anyone saw me along the way, fine. I doubt it, so you see I have no alibi."

His tone mocking, he added, "And when Guthrie got his just deserts the weekend before last, I happened to be on a retreat in the Blue Mountains at Wisdom Lodge. Very soothing, but everyone on the retreat goes off and does his or her own thing, so I hardly saw anyone except at mealtimes. Vegetarian, of course."

"Of course," said Carol.

"It's quite a drive to Dubbo," said Fitch, "but I suppose I could have sneaked away. You'll have to explain how I knew where Guthrie was at that particular time. I hardly had time to stalk him, did I?"

It was interesting, Carol thought, how keen Gerald Fitch was to invite examination of his movements. She wondered if he was truly eager to be on a short list of suspects. Carol had seen this before — people so drawn by the notoriety that they even got to the point of confessing to crimes they hadn't committed.

When Carol and Anne got up to leave, Fitch saw them down the steps to the street. "Inspector," he said, "I doubt you'll solve the Banning murder." With a touch of drama, he paused, then added, "Or the others to come."

In the car, Anne said, "What's with that guy? He's practically begging us to investigate him."

"For one thing, I think Fitch wants the publicity, but perhaps he also wants to deflect attention from someone else in the organization. We need a membership list. Also, contact Cardover's former personal assistant. Marcie Evans is her name, and maybe she kept a file of protesters similar to Valerie Rule's."

"You know," said Anne, "I could almost imagine rubbing out someone like Banning myself. He's done so much damage."

Carol looked at her sideways. "You didn't murder him, did you, Anne?" she asked. "Because if you did, I'll have to take you off the case."

Loren Reece was exactly on time. Carol had been replying to one of Aunt Sarah's voluminous e-mails. She shut down the computer and got up to greet the journalist, thinking how she looked like a successful executive in the gray silk suit she was wearing. She carried a slim navy blue attaché case. "Good morning, Carol."

Noting the informal use of her name, Carol replied dryly, "Good morning, Loren."

Loren laughed. "Well, the pleasantries are over with."

Carol gestured her to a chair and retreated behind her desk, watching as Loren took out a miniature recorder. She put it on Carol's desk. "Do you mind if I record this?"

Carol nodded reluctantly. "Will this take long?"

"No, it's only a preliminary interview."

"Preliminary?"

Raising her dark eyebrows, the American said, "Didn't Superintendent Edgar tell you?"

With a feeling of foreboding, Carol said, "Tell me what?"

"That he's agreed I sort of ride along with you. Follow your investigations for a few days. He said he'd brief you about it."

"It's the first I've heard."

Loren was contrite. "I'm sorry, Carol. I thought you knew."

"I'm afraid it isn't possible."

"Are you sure?" Loren cocked her head. "I wouldn't get in the way, and I'm the soul of discretion."

Thinking how typical it was of the super to agree to such a thing without consulting her, Carol said, without meaning it, "Maybe we can work something out."

"I hope so." Her tone was warm and friendly, and Carol frowned, thinking that this was a woman who would get her own way without even seeming to try.

The red light on the recorder blinked on, and

Loren began to ask a series of innocuous questions about Carol's background and career. "I'm sure you know all this already," Carol said. "I believe you assured me last night that your researched your subjects thoroughly."

"Just relaxing you," said Loren cheerfully. "The hard stuff comes later."

Although silently cursing Superintendent Edgar that he'd agreed to give this American journalist such free rein, Carol found herself enjoying the fielding of the questions pitched at her. Many of them were thoughtful queries, needing close consideration. She was almost disappointed when Loren looked at her watch and said, "Okay, time's up."

She flipped her notebook shut, packed up the recorder, and stood. "I hope you note that I've been expeditious," she said, grinning. "Are you sure you're not free for lunch?"

"I'm sure."

Loren hesitated, then said, "Carol, I am sorry about this mix-up. If you'd check with the superintendent, perhaps we can arrange something that will be acceptable to you."

"I'll certainly be speaking with him."

Obviously amused at Carol's sardonic tone, Loren said, "I can imagine. I'll be in touch, okay?"

"Where are you staying?" Carol asked, unaccountably curious.

"The Ritz-Carlton in Macquarie Street."

Carol raised a mental eyebrow. A five-star hotel. International journalism obviously paid better than the local kind. "I'll leave a message for you there," she said.

After Loren Reece had gone, Carol sat playing with her gold pen. She had been feeling isolated, alone. Now, in some vague way, there was a possibility, however tenuous, of a new friendship.

CHAPTER NINE

Carol came out of Superintendent Edgar's office in a cold rage. "It wasn't clear to you?" he'd said when she'd complained about the promises made to Loren Reece about access to Carol's work. "Well, Carol, you'll just have to go along with it. I'm sure the woman won't be as intrusive as you expect."

When Sam Goolwa stopped her in the hallway, she snapped, "What?"

He looked so taken aback at her tone that felt a stab of guilt. "Sorry. What was it you wanted?"

"Anne asked me to look at the names posted on the Gaia Web site to check what killed them. I've been on the Internet all morning, and I've got most of them pegged."

Carol scanned the page he'd handed her. "Good work."

A quick smile flickered across Goolwa's face, then he was all business again. "You'll see I've put them in categories, and indicated the way they died." A note of humor crept into his voice as he added, "A lot of them seem to have more bad luck than your average person."

"Come into my office and tell me your thoughts."

Clearly pleased to be asked his opinion, he followed her through the door, then stood irresolutely until she gestured for him to sit.

She nodded encouragement, and he began. "There are eighteen names now that Mr. Cardover has been added. Of those eighteen, five had heart attacks or strokes, three people were murdered by gunshots, one suicided, one had a shotgun go off in his face while he was climbing through a fence, and one collected a bullet while spotlighting kangaroos. Then there were two who died of cancer. The remaining five had accidents."

"What sort of accidents?"

Sam Goolwa, Carol noted, didn't need to refer to written material. He answered immediately. "One had a fall at home down a flight of stairs, a woman in Italy was electrocuted, there were two fatal car accidents, and the last one, an American, fell off a cliff in the Grand Canyon."

"How many deaths would you say were suspicious?"

"Could be murder, you mean? On the surface, the three who were deliberately shot are fair dinkum, but I'd put in the possible homicide group maybe three or four of the others. One heart attack victim was only thirty-three. I'll have to get more details on how each of them died and if there were witnesses."

"Make it a priority."

He jumped up, "You got it!"

She was still smiling at his enthusiasm when Bourke came in. "Something to wipe that smile of your face," he said. "I'm just back from the morgue. Cardover was injected with a lethal dose of anesthetic. He'd had so many procedures to take blood samples et cetera during his hospital stay, it wasn't surprising that no one noticed an extra puncture mark."

Carol realized she wasn't surprised. The sense of urgency that galvanized her when she was on a challenging case was growing more intense. Filled with a spurt of energy, she said, "Let's get on top of this quickly, Mark. Li and Standish have interviewed the hospital staff. Have a look at their reports and see if there's anything. And what about Nurse Slade?"

"Ah," said Bourke, "now there's an interesting woman. This fascinating fact wasn't in Dr. Olson's file, but the healing hands of our Marilyn Slade were accused of mercy killing some eight years ago in Melbourne. Two patients, one in the last stages of cancer, the other a stroke victim."

"I presume she was found not guilty?"

Bourke spread his hands. "The case never came to trial, for lack of evidence. I only picked it up because Slade had used the head of nursing staff at a big Melbourne hospital as one of her work references when she applied for the job at Wallhaven. When I called it was immediately clear the head had no time for Slade, so she was delighted to dish the dirt."

"Seems like Dr. Olson never checked that particular reference," said Carol, adding, amused, "If Phyllis Cardover gets hold of that information, she'll sue the pants off the hospital."

"I've asked for details of the case to be sent up from Melbourne," said Bourke. "If the modus operandi matches, maybe we have a turquoise-and-white angel of death just waiting to be arrested."

"Are you saying that Cardover's murder within a day of Banning's being shot is just an unfortunate coincidence?"

"I grant you it looks odd to have the two principals of Banning and Cardover offed within twenty-four hours of each other." He went on playfully. "You know, Marilyn Slade's bio says she grew up in a country town, so maybe she's a recreational shooter. She pops Banning in the head Thursday morning, then uses a more discreet method to off Cardover the next day." His smile widened. "I'm pleased with that scenario. What do you think?"

"I think a convincing motive would help, Mark," Carol said dryly.

After he'd gone, on impulse she picked up the phone and called the Ritz-Carlton hotel. Loren Reece wasn't in her room, so Carol left a voice-mail message to say that she'd spoken to the superintendent, and Loren would be able to accompany Carol at certain times.

Very restricted times, she thought as she replaced the receiver.

Very late in the afternoon Carol held a briefing with the officers she had assigned to the Banning and Cardover cases. She noticed that when Sam Goolwa came into the briefing room and looked for a seat, Constable Miles Li quickly put papers down on the empty chair next to him, apparently to prevent Goolwa from sitting beside him.

She succinctly summed up the overall status of each case and commented on the possibility that the same perpetrator had committed both murders. Bourke summarized Standish and Li's investigation of the hospital staff, which in essence had turned up nothing of use. The member of the nursing staff who had been with Nurse Slade in the corridor had noticed no one near Cardover's room. Background checks had turned up one orderly who had a minor drug charge, and another who had been arrested for disturbing the peace.

Standish said, "The security at Wallhaven Hospital is pretty lax. Miles and I managed to walk in through the loading dock at the back without anyone paying any attention to us, so I reckon someone wearing the right hospital uniform wouldn't have any trouble at all. What's more, there's a staff change room on the bottom floor that's never locked, so a perp could nick a uniform at any time and use it later."

Anne had tracked down Marcie Evans, Cardover's personal assistant. The woman, Anne said, was adamant that she had never bothered to keep any threatening letters sent to Eric Cardover, announcing that she put them through the shredder the moment she realized what they were. She had never heard of an organization called Gaia's Revenge, or anyone called Gerald Fitch.

"Ms. Evans is very angry about being fired," said Anne, "so she was more than happy to repeat rumors and make allegations." She checked her notes. "Specifically, she named a Phoebe Yarmelle as Banning's current girlfriend. She said everyone knew about it, even Banning's wife. Then she bad-mouthed Cardover's son, Jonathan. Since he was the one who fired her, perhaps we should take it with a grain of salt, but she swore there were several violent arguments between father and son in the week before the elder Cardover had a stroke. The bone of contention was Jonathan Cardover's position in the firm. He wanted to move up and take some of his father's responsibilities, but Eric Cardover would have none of it."

"Okay," said Carol, "we need someone to check out this Phoebe Yarmelle. Miles, will you do that? Also ask around in Banning and Cardover and see if anyone else heard these arguments between Cardover and his son. Anne, check where Fitch was on Friday morning. If we're lucky, he had a dentist appointment, so he can't lay claim to Cardover's murder."

Bourke reported on Valerie Rule's whereabouts for the relevant time periods. Several witnesses confirmed that she'd been into work early at the Banning & Cardover offices both days. Her personal record was spotless. No arrests, no late payments on credit cards or loans, in fact, no outstanding debts. "The woman's a saint. Not even a speeding ticket."

Bourke added, "She did tell us one lie though. Seems she knew the name Gaia's Revenge because Gerald Fitch stormed into Banning and Cardover and confronted her boss in his office. She was embarrassed to admit that anyone could get past her."

"Anne, anything new on Gaia's Revenge?" Carol asked.

"Not much. As far as the Sydney branch is concerned, there doesn't seem to be a bank account in the organization's name. Gerald Fitch pays the rent on the Glebe offices with a personal check each month. People in the therapy practice downstairs in the same building say that there are always people coming and going, but there's no way to find out the membership numbers or even how the branch is organized."

Carol looked to Goolwa. "Sam? You've got something on the overseas end?"

"Not much more than Anne has been able to get on the Aussie branch. Gaia's Revenge is a really shadowy operation. The headquarters are in New York, but it's pretty much the same thing — a little office run by one person, a woman called Bonnie d'Arlene, who seems to be the overall leader. They reach most people through their Web site, which is a comprehensive one, constantly updated with environmental news from around the world."

"Find out what you can about this Bonnie d'Arlene," said Carol to Goolwa. "It might be useful if I had a conversation with her about her international branches."

After discussing further details of the investigation

and allocating duties, Carol ended the session. She gestured for Miles Li to stay behind. He was slightly built, and looked very young. His straight black hair fell over his forehead, and he had the idiosyncratic habit of brushing it back with two extended fingers.

Waiting until the others had filed out, she said to him, "How do you get on with Sam Goolwa?"

He looked at her warily. "Okay."

"He's new. I was wondering how he's fitting in."

"Okay," he repeated.

"So there are no problems?"

Li looked uncomfortable. "Not really." When Carol remained silent with an interrogative expression on her face, Li said, "Well, he *is* an Abo."

Controlling the flash of anger she felt at this derogatory appellation, Carol said, "And that makes a difference?"

Li had obviously realized he'd said the wrong thing. "No, it doesn't make a difference, of course."

Just as annoyed at this prevarication as with his use of a disparaging slang term for *Aborigine*, Carol said, "We're a team. It's the only way to get results, and it won't work if some of us are treated like outsiders."

Li's expression was carefully neutral. "I understand," he said.

What made it even more unforgivable, Carol thought, was that Miles Li had migrated with his parents from Hong Kong when he was a kid. She imagined that Li himself had experienced some discrimination because he looked different, both when he was growing up and after he became an officer. The

Police Service still had a cadre of old-time cops who were not noted for their enlightened views on minorities.

"Would you be happy if someone called you a Chink?" she demanded.

"God, no!"

"Then don't call Sam Goolwa an Abo. To his face or to anyone else. Understood?"

Dismissed, he hurried from the room. Carol shook her head. She'd seen it before, but she never could understand how a member of one minority, knowing full well what it was like to be treated badly because of ethnicity, would perpetuate the same injustice on someone else.

"We've been informed that your son, David, has been charged with a serious drug offense," said the reporter on the line, a tenacious man she recognized from past encounters. "Would you care to comment?"

Carol knew the game. She was supposed to be goaded into denying the charge was a serious one, which would, of course, confirm that David had been charged with something.

"I never comment on personal matters, Tom," she said. "You know that."

This was the third call on this subject she'd parried today, including one from Madeline Shipley of the television newsmagazine, *The Shipley Report*. Even though Madeline was a friend, and had essentially called to be supportive about David, Carol had stonewalled her the same way as she had the others.

"Then perhaps," said Tom Keys, "you *would* care

to comment on the Banning murder? Is it true you suspect it was a professional hit? That a twenty-two was used?"

Not matter how tight the lid on information, some of it always leaked out. Carol said, "It's very early in our investigation. A statement will be released shortly."

"How shortly?"

"Tom, I don't know." She could hear the whiplash of impatience in her voice.

"Hey, Carol," he said, "I'm only doing my job."

Tom Keys was an investigative journalist who was legendary for his network of informants in every field. Struck by the thought that she might be able to use him to advantage, Carol said, "Have you ever heard of a group called Gaia's Revenge?"

"How do you spell that?"

Once he'd got it correct, he said, "Okay, what about this group?"

"They're extreme environmentalists. I believe they've been making threats to the heads of different companies. I'd like to know what you turn up."

"Eco-terrorists, eh?" He sounded satisfied, and Carol knew that he'd made the simple connection that Gaia's Revenge had threatened Walter Banning. "I'll get back to you, Carol. And thanks."

Loren Reece called back just as Carol was packing up to go home. "I got your message, and I'm delighted we can work together."

"Work together?"

Loren chuckled. "Relax, I'm not going to be running around solving crimes for you. How about dinner tomorrow night? I've got a sinful expense account, so I'm paying. We can establish guidelines so I don't disrupt your job for you. Please say yes."

Carol hesitated for a moment, then said, "That would be fine." They established where and when, and Loren rang off.

Carol caught Bourke as he was leaving. "Mark, I want you to run a full check on Loren Reece."

"Why? What's she done?"

"Not a thing that I know off, but the super has arranged for her to have access to our offices, and I don't like the idea that someone I know nothing about is snooping around."

"Okay," said Bourke. "I haven't met the woman, but Pat likes her a lot."

"Pat would like anyone a lot who bought paintings from her gallery," said Carol.

Bearing in mind Superintendent Edgar's mantra, "Keep me informed," Carol made her way to his office before she left for the day. She was half hoping he wouldn't be there, but he was on the phone, lounging back comfortably in his chair. He waved her to a seat and continued his conversation, which appeared to be about the organization of a fishing weekend in the Snowy River area.

Watching him talk, she felt the sting of real dislike. She hadn't played being one of the boys to get her where she was in her career, but had relied on sheer hard work. It didn't hurt, of course, that her early mentor had been the police commissioner, and she knew that Edgar and others like him resented that connection.

Carol was convinced he'd do his best to block her promotion, should she apply for consideration, especially as he was almost certainly irked by the recent elevation of two women to the high position of detective superintendent.

Chief Inspector Ashton. That sounded good to Carol. And there were precedents for her to leap more than one rank. *Superintendent Ashton?* That had an even better ring to it. She glanced at Edgar's smug expression and smiled to herself. The very thought of Carol having the rank of superintendent would give him apoplexy.

Still, she wasn't sure if she wanted the problems that a display of ambition would bring. She enjoyed her present job and did it well. But didn't she need new challenges, new directions in her life? At one time she'd even considered leaving the police and doing something else, but she had quickly shelved that idea. There was nothing else she could think of that would give her the pleasure in work that she had now.

Edgar was droning on interminably about arcane fishing trivia, so Carol let her mind wander back to the Banning and Cardover murders. Was the link between the crimes personal or business? Or both? On the surface, the one person who seemed to gain the most was Jonathan Cardover, presuming that his mother wanted him installed at the top of the firm, and Felicity Banning, with her controlling interest, agreed.

And Jonathan would fit in with the problem of the Rolls' open window, which had been nagging Carol. Would you open a window to a stranger who had suddenly appeared in your garage? Surely Banning would have been more cautious. In those circumstances, Carol thought he would have been more likely to stamp on the accelerator and reverse out into the street. But if it were Jonathan at the window, of course Banning would put the window down to see what in the hell his partner's son was doing there.

As to the weapon, for an ordinary person handguns were difficult to obtain, though anything could be bought for a price on Sydney's streets. Perhaps a sawed-off twenty-two rifle? There were hundreds of thousands of those around, surviving the strict gun laws imposed after the massacre in Tasmania where a heavily armed and deranged man had committed mass murder.

What if the killer had been Gerald Fitch of Gaia's Revenge? Carol couldn't imagine that Walter Banning would have opened his window to the activist who had confronted him in the firm's offices only a few months before.

Carol recreated the scene in her mind's eye. The double garage was tidy, with a workbench running along the back wall. Felicity Banning's blue BMW sat beside her husband's black Rolls-Royce. The entrance to the internal stairs was in the kitchen above, and for security the door automatically locked when it closed behind Banning. Anyone entering the house from the garage had to have the numbers to open the combination lock.

She could see Banning, wearing the charcoal gray suit Carol later saw splashed with his blood, coming down the stairs. He opened the driver's door of the Rolls, slung his briefcase onto the passenger seat, and slid behind the wheel. Turning the ignition key activated all the locks, so he was secure. Then, before he could put the car into gear, someone appeared beside the car. Carol could visualize the person tapping on the window, or perhaps mouthing, *I have to tell you something*. And Banning had obediently opened it, and died. Surely it had been someone he knew and had no reason to fear.

Her thoughts drifted to Felicity Banning. She'd said good-bye to him in the kitchen, so why didn't she hear the two shots a few minutes later? In her statement she'd said that about half an hour after she thought Banning had left, she'd come down into the garage to get meat for that night's dinner out of a freezer and found the Rolls still there, its motor running. Her grief and desolation at her husband's death had been convincing, but Carol reminded herself that this was no guarantee of innocence.

What linked Walter Banning's murder to his partner's? She asked herself the key question, *Who benefits?*

Superintendent Edgar broke into her thoughts by slamming down his phone. "Well, Carol?"

She gave him a brief rundown of the two investigations. As she spoke, his expression grew darker. "Don't let this drag on," he said. "The longer the media have it, the more fun they'll have."

Carol barely resisted snapping at him that the murders had occurred respectively four and three days before, so she had hardly had time to complete her initial investigations. "Do you want a media conference?" she said with polite inquiry.

There was a measure of malice in her question. Carol was accustomed to media attention, having often been used as the police spokesperson because of her communication skills. Edgar craved the limelight, but he was a poor performer in front of a camera, and he knew it. On those occasions when he'd appeared on television news she'd seen his thick neck swell as his face reddened. He was inclined to waffle, stumble over words, and generally make a poor impression.

Evidence of a struggle was on his face. She knew he ardently desired the exposure, but, equally, he didn't want to make a fool of himself.

"Bit premature," he said. "Let's wait a few days."

CHAPTER TEN

Carol had hardly put her things down on Wednesday morning when Tom Keys called her. "I've got the good oil on Gaia's Revenge. What've you got for me, Carol?"

"You first, Tom. You're not above bluffing me, I know."

He gave a hoarse whiskey-and-cigarettes laugh. "Get your pen. I've got a name for you."

She fished around for her gold pen. Unscrewing the cap, she said, "Okay."

"Phoebe Yarmelle." He spelled it out. "Got it?"

Carol looked at the name she'd written with astonishment. It was Banning's girlfriend. It was impossible there would be two women with such an unusual name. "Yes?" she said to encourage Tom Keys to go on.

He laughed again. "Bit of a surprise for you, Carol? I believe she was the late unlamented Banning's lover."

"So I've been told."

"About four months ago she joined Gaia's Revenge. Cut quite a swath through the ranks, I believe. Brought lots of money with her and, she said, 'a burning desire to punish the planet's despoilers.' I'm quoting directly from a contact here."

"Who is your contact?"

"Sorry, Carol, no can do. I can tell you, however, that Phoebe was kicked out of Gaia when they found out she was a spy for Banning. There was quite a nasty scene with threats flowing freely from both sides."

"How extreme were these threats?"

"You'll have to ask Phoebe. Now, where's my payoff?"

Carol gave him those details she knew either she or Edgar would be releasing at a media conference in the next few days, including the fact that the death of Banning's partner was suspicious enough to warrant a postmortem. She commented on how Banning & Cardover had been the target of concentrated attacks from various environmental groups, and that she would be looking into any definite threats that Banning had received.

Tom Keys was pleased. "Good stuff," he said. "I'll be calling tomorrow for more."

"Only if you have something startling for me."

"I'm working on it," Keys said. "In the meantime, I do have one tidbit you might like to know."

"I'll bite. What is it?"

"Fitch, the guy who runs Gaia's Revenge? He's finessed himself a spot on Madeline Shipley's show." He gave a hoarse laugh that degenerated into a violent coughing fit.

"You'll have to cut down the smoking, Tom."

"Never," he said, breathless. Recovering, he went on, "You've got to admire Fitch. He's milking the situation for a lot of free publicity. He even offered me a print exclusive on his informed view of eco-terrorist activities."

"Did you take him up on it?"

"Trade secret," said Keys. "You'll know if you see it in the paper."

After he'd hung up, Carol went to find Miles Li, but he'd already left to interview Banning's girlfriend. She decided to let it go, waiting to see what Phoebe Yarmelle told him before arranging to interview the woman herself.

She placed a call to Madeline Shipley, but she wasn't in her office, so Carol left a message with her assistant. Then she sat back to consider Gerald Fitch. Keys was right about the free publicity — *The Shipley Report* had very high ratings, and if Tom Keys took up Fitch's offer as well, the exposure that both Gaia's Revenge and Fitch himself would gain would be considerable. On a hunch, she made a few quick calls to media contacts and found that Fitch had been shopping his story widely. She thought of making a call to Fitch himself, but decided not to do so until she'd spoken to Madeline.

Late in the morning Bourke brought her a mug of black coffee and sat down to report on Nurse Slade. "Her activities in Melbourne were very straightforward. There's no hard proof, but it seems obvious that she disconnected the life support systems for two of her comatose patients. Neither of them had any hope of recovery, so apparently she just hurried things along."

"That's no excuse."

"Maybe not, Carol, but it's not the same as the malice aforethought of setting up a lethal injection. Besides, I can't find any motive for her to kill Cardover. Can you?"

Carol shrugged. "Okay, I concede Marilyn Slade's a long shot."

As he stood to go he said, "And here's the information you wanted on Loren Reece. The premier's publicity agent faxed me her C.V., and I got a mate in the LAPD to do a quick search in the States. She's quite aboveboard. I've read the travel articles she did last year on Australia. She's a good journalist and has a flair for pinning down a place in a few sentences."

As she sipped her coffee she read through the information Bourke had given her. Loren Reece was the only child of William and Robyn Reece, both now deceased. She'd been born in Yorba Linda, Los Angeles. She graduated from UCLA and had started her journalistic career on a small local paper in New Mexico, working her way up to prestigious national newspapers. Then she struck out on her own, establishing herself as a highly regarded freelance writer specializing in travel and women's issues. There was an impressive list of her published articles, plus glowing recommendations from various editors and fellow journalists.

Loren Reece had never been arrested in the United States, although she had been detained for two days in Mexico while researching an exposé of corruption in the Mexican law enforcement agencies. She was in excellent health, had a triple-A credit rating, and maintained an apartment in an upscale area of New York City, although she was often out of the country. There was no record of her ever being married.

As Carol folded the pages and put them away in the top drawer of her desk, she thought of how personal privacy had vanished in recent years. Anyone with access to a computer could troll the world to find out basic facts, and it only needed a little more skill to access information on bank accounts, personal health records and property holdings.

It was an uncomfortable thought to consider that it was very likely Loren had done a similar search on her. What was there that Carol wouldn't want her to know? Her salary? The second mortgage she'd taken out to fund the alterations to her house? The fact that she was gay? With sardonic amusement, Carol admitted to herself that she was quite content to search through other people's private lives, but she resented like hell anyone looking into hers.

She went in search of Sam Goolwa and found him hunched over a computer monitor staring at the screen. He started when she said, "How are you going on the Gaia list? Turned up any more murders?"

"Not really." He sounded disappointed. "I mean, some of these deaths look suspicious to me, but there's nothing to prove they're deliberate killings."

Carol had to grin at his chagrin. "Would you rather there was an international mass murderer loose?"

He laughed. "Well, no, of course not."

She peered over his shoulder at the screen. "Which do you consider suspicious deaths?"

"I had hopes for the guy who had a heart attack in his early thirties, but he had a family history of heart trouble. The deaths that look like accidents, however, are worth a second look. For example, one guy broke his neck falling down a flight of stairs in London, and there were no witnesses. Then there's the Italian mink breeder who was electrocuted, the chemical company executive who fell off a cliff into the Grand Canyon, and the oil company CEO who blew his head off with a shotgun while climbing through a fence."

"If a hit man exists, he's certainly going for variety," said Carol. "However, there's a good chance all these are just what they seem to be — accidents."

"Yeah," said Goolwa glumly.

"Sam, you've done good work that may be helpful in the future, but now we need to concentrate on whether the Gaia group here had anything to do with Banning's or Cardover's deaths."

As she went to go, he said, "You know you asked me to check on Bonnie d'Arlene in the New York headquarters of Gaia's Revenge? She's in Australia."

Carol turned to look at him. "She's here?"

"Sure is." He consulted his scribbled notes. "Came in on a tourist visa three weeks ago and gave her address as a hotel in Bondi. But she's long gone from there, and there's no record of her leaving the country. Who knows where she is?"

It was intriguing that a visit from the highest ranking member of Gaia apparently coincided with deaths celebrated on the organization's Web site. "Sam, find out anything you can about this woman's background. Leave Fitch to me."

Before she reached her office she caught sight of Miles Li and called him over. "How did the interview with Phoebe Yarmelle go?"

"Haven't typed my notes up yet, but I can tell you right now she only said one interesting thing, which was that Banning had guaranteed Phoebe he'd told his wife he wanted a divorce and that he'd already got a lawyer working on it."

"When did she last see Banning?"

Li pushed the hair off his forehead. "The night before he died. They had dinner together at her flat, then he left to go home about ten-thirty. I asked if he seemed worried or preoccupied, and she said it was just the same as usual."

"Where was she when he was killed?"

"Sleeping in, she said. Had a lazy morning alone, and only found out what had happened when she turned on the radio at lunchtime."

"Phoebe Yarmelle didn't tell you that Banning asked her a few months back to infiltrate the Gaia's Revenge organization?"

Obviously taken aback, he said, "Not a word."

"What else did you get?"

"Only that Banning paid the rent for the flat. It's one of those posh places at Kirribilli. And she went on with all this stuff about how his wife didn't understand him and how she really loved him." Li's world-weary tone indicated his scorn for this well-worn stratagem.

"Do you have her telephone number?"

"Sure. She gave me her card."

Carol looked at the cardboard rectangle with a raised eyebrow. "Interior decorator?"

"That's what she says she does."

Picking up the nearest phone, Carol punched in the numbers. "Ms. Yarmelle? This is Detective Inspector Ashton. I'm in charge of the investigation into Walter Banning's death. I know you've already spoken with Constable Li, but some new information has come to light. I wonder if you'd be available to come here now if I sent Constable Li to pick you up?"

She listened to the high voice at the other end of the line agreeing to her request, thanked her, and put down the receiver. "Back you go, Miles," she said. "She'll be waiting at the apartment entrance in half an hour." As he turned to go, she added, "You know, I rather think she fancies you." His expression sent her chuckling all the way to her office.

An hour later Miles Li was back with Phoebe Yarmelle. She wasn't what Carol had envisaged. Carol knew she was in her mid-twenties, although she looked much younger. She was attractive, but not remarkably so, with an abundance of thick chestnut hair that framed her intense face. Her eyes were her best feature, being large and startlingly blue. She wasn't model skinny, but was quite well covered. A comfortable body, Carol thought. Phoebe was wearing the latest in fashion gear, although on her it seemed not quite appropriate, as though she were a kid dressing up. Part of this impression came from her high, light voice, and also from the fact that she was very short, although she'd added considerably to her height with heels so high that Carol was fascinated to see her walk on them without turning an ankle.

Carol gestured for Miles Li to sit in on the interview, then put on an understanding smile as she said to Phoebe, "You must be very upset."

Phoebe dumped her large shoulder bag on the floor and flung herself in the nearest chair, giving her short leather skirt a tug in an attempt to preserve her modesty. "Too right I am! Wally was that good to me, I don't reckon I'll find another bloke like him, at least not for a long while."

"He paid for your apartment?"

"Yeah, six months in advance." Concern filled her face. "There's four months left. The wife won't pitch me out, will she? Like, Wally said he was changing his will, just in case something happened to him, so she wouldn't get everything."

She wriggled around in the chair and gave another abortive tug to her skirt. "Don't think he got round to it, though. He said the will would have to be redone once the divorce went through, anyway."

Carol wondered what a man in Banning's position would see in someone like Phoebe Yarmelle. It was surprising to her that he hadn't gone for a trophy female, someone svelte and sophisticated that he could show off. But then, Phoebe had her own unique charm. Carol liked her artlessness and energy and lack of self-consciousness.

Phoebe said, "She hates me, you know."

"Mr. Banning's wife, you mean?"

"Yeah, Felicity." She pronounced the name with disdain. "She came over one night and fronted me in

109

my own place, would you believe?" A grin appeared as she said, "Should have heard what she called me. Language even *I* wouldn't use. Like, she was screaming so loud I was scared someone in the building would hear and call the cops."

Phoebe was convincing, but Carol wanted verification. She said, "Do you know if anyone did hear the argument?"

A shrug. "Search me. I got some funny looks the next morning." Her face warmed with another smile as she added, "Of course, I often get funny looks. Don't ask me why."

"After we finish, I want you to give Constable Li all the information you can about this confrontation."

Phoebe shot Li a cheerful smile. "Be a pleasure, but there was more than one. You want that too?"

Amused, Carol assured her she wanted to know about all the times Phoebe and Felicity Banning had met. Then she asked, "I believe you joined Gaia's Revenge a few months back."

Phoebe tilted her head. "What's it to you?"

"Did Mr. Banning ask you to join the group to see what was going on, or was it all your idea?"

"What if I say I was just doing my bit to save the world?" Phoebe's expression was mischievous. "I donated plenty of money to the cause, you know."

"Your money?"

"No way! Wally's."

"It's only," said Carol, "we're wondering if someone in Gaia's Revenge may be implicated in Mr. Banning's murder."

Phoebe immediately sobered. "Could be. The head guy's name is Fitch. You know him?"

"We've met," said Carol.

"Looks harmless, doesn't he? Well, he's *not*. He bluffed his way into Wally's office at work, and told Wally he was going to be killed. Actually, he said he was going to be executed, like Wally was a criminal or something."

"What made you turn up as a new recruit for Gaia's Revenge?"

Phoebe leaned on Carol's desk, saying in a confiding tone, "Wally was packing death, see. Scared shitless. I reminded him people had threatened to kill him like a thousand times before, and nothing had happened, but he said this time was different. To make him feel better, I said to him, why don't I bluff my way into the group and have a look-see what's going on. I wasn't really serious about it, but Wally latched on to the idea, so I had to go ahead with it."

"You had no trouble joining?" Carol asked.

"Not really. I said all the right things about whales and rain forest and how big business was fucking everything up, and that convinced them I was on the up-and-up. It was quite fun at first, sort of like being a spy, but then it got pretty boring with everyone going on and on about pollution and all that stuff. I went along with it all, but I thought they were just a joke, and I told Wally so. But then I found out that they weren't really a joke at all. And right after that, someone telephoned Gaia and dobbed me in, so they got rid of me."

Phoebe leaned forward, as if to convince Carol she had something important to impart. "This Gaia lot, they're killing people all over the world. And the bastards did Wally in, just like Fitch said they would."

Convinced that Phoebe would have seen the list on the Web site, Carol said, "What do you base this on?

That the organization had a category called *Notable Deletions* on the Internet?"

"Got it from the horse's mouth," said Phoebe, clearly indignant. "Fitch was big-noting himself, trying to impress me because he thought I was a bit keen on him. I played along, and he talked too much. Simple as that."

"Did he name anyone?"

"As if he would! Even Fitch isn't that stupid. He told me Gaia had hired an assassin. That's what he called him, an assassin, as if the guy was a step above your ordinary killer. Fitch said that part of members' dues went to pay this person's salary, like it was a regular job."

Carol said, "Have you ever heard of Bonnie d'Arlene?"

"Big Bonnie? She started the whole thing. Runs Gaia from New York."

"Did you know that Ms. d'Arlene is presently in Australia?"

"Yeah? Nobody told me." Phoebe pointed a scarlet forefinger at Carol. "If she's here, she's the one you need to look up, Inspector. A real maniac. I've seen her tapes and read the stuff she writes, and I can tell you that she believes anything goes when it comes to saving the world."

She punctuated this with a definitive nod, then collected her things. "I'll be off, then."

"I'm afraid you'll have to give a formal statement before you go," said Carol. "And perhaps you'll make it clear why you didn't contact the police when you realized that members of Gaia's Revenge were capable of murder, and had specifically threatened Mr. Banning."

Phoebe screwed up her face. "Wally wouldn't let me. He told me he couldn't afford to have the cops nosing round his business. He said he had everything under control, because he was getting a bodyguard. A professional." She threw up her hands. "But it was too late. Before he got around to hiring anyone, they shot him."

Her tone severe, Carol said, "You should have come forward with this information the moment you heard that Mr. Banning had been murdered. Why didn't you?"

Phoebe gave her a sheepish smile. "Thought I could stay out of it, didn't I? But I had to do something, so you'll be getting a letter from me in the mail, probably tomorrow, telling you all about it. I didn't sign it, of course."

"Constable Li will take a written statement from you. Please go into as much detail as you can about everything you know about the group and Mr. Fitch."

"Sure thing. And do you want the membership records too?"

Carol blinked. "You have copies?"

Phoebe was pleased with herself. "I don't do things by halves," she said, "and I'm pretty good with a computer. I copied all their files, and you can have them, if you like." She rummaged around in her capacious bag. "Not that they're any big secret, anyway. Fitch sold the names and addresses to make money. Mainly to companies that make those awful footwear and hiking gear, and all that organic sort of thing." She handed Carol a bundle of crumpled sheets.

"Don't know how the ecology types wear them," Phoebe said. "Those ugly thick sandals with their great fat straps." She looked approvingly at her stiletto heels. "You need something good on your feet, you know."

Madeline Shipley called back after lunch. "Sorry, Carol, I hate to keep my favorite detective inspector waiting, but I was on location. What can I do for you?"

"Gerald Fitch," said Carol.

Madeline gave her signature husky laugh. "You've obviously heard I'm doing an item on him. He and his environmental group may be a bit way out, but that makes for a good story."

"And just what particular story is Mr. Fitch telling?"

Clearly amused at Carol's acerbic tone, Madeline said, "I'm interviewing him tomorrow night about the quaintly named Gaia's Revenge, and he's promised some bombshells. You can get the general idea from the promos tonight if you watch my show." She paused, then added, "Carol, tell me you *do* watch my show."

Carol could imagine Madeline's face glowing with the same enthusiasm that she used as a potent force on television screens five times a week. She wasn't merely run-of-the-mill television attractive. Madeline Shipley was outstandingly beautiful, and this, combined with obvious intelligence and good humor, had allowed her program to consistently hold high ratings in a very competitive time slot.

Carol said, "What sort of bombshells?"

"I was going to call you," said Madeline. "But not until after the show aired tomorrow. Fitch says there's a worldwide conspiracy to murder people he terms environmental vandals."

"You've seen the Gaia Web site?"

"Of course. My researchers checked it out right away."

"Fitch will merely be repeating the names on the Internet list," said Carol. "I've had someone reviewing the cases, and there's just no way they were all murdered."

"I don't know why you say that with such confidence," said Madeline. "I mean, three of these so-called vandals died here in Australia. Correct me if I'm wrong, but aren't you investigating two of them as murders? And the 'roo shooting case also looks mighty suspicious, even to me."

Carol frowned at the mention of Edward Guthrie's death. Obviously Fitch had mentioned it to Madeline. The media loved a conspiracy theory and would seize the opportunity to tie Guthrie's shooting to the murders of Banning and Cardover, even if there was no hard evidence a connection existed.

"Guthrie's death has been ruled an accident," Carol said. "There's nothing there."

Madeline gave a low chuckle. "You're not hiding something from me, are you, Carol?"

CHAPTER ELEVEN

In the late afternoon Carol and Bourke went to the Banning & Cardover building in the city. Jonathan Cardover had proved difficult to pin down, and he had agreed to see them with obvious reluctance.

A thin young woman wearing a micro skirt and a shallow smile ushered them into a room that Carol knew had been the elder Cardover's office. The furniture was heavy and dark, and most of the walls were covered with shelves holding leather-backed books.

Jonathan Cardover, sitting behind a massive desk,

did not get up to greet them. Seeing Carol eyeing the room, he said, "This is all changing, as soon as I can rip out this stuff. My father had no sense of the modern, in business or in furnishings."

"Thank you for making time to see us," said Carol, as if Cardover had been fully cooperative. She sat in one of the square chairs upholstered in dark green leather that faced the desk.

Cardover waited until Bourke was seated, then snapped, "I'm extremely busy, Inspector Ashton. I really can't spare the time, so I'd appreciate it if we kept this short."

He had the loud, bullying voice of one accustomed to getting his own way. Carol looked him over critically. His black hair was thick and his face, somewhat marred by a petulant set to his lips, was strong. He was carrying far too much weight for his moderate height, and, although a comparatively young man, he was developing jowls. His neck bulged over the tight collar of his striped shirt.

"Your father was murdered, Mr. Cardover. I imagine you want to see the person responsible brought to justice."

"Of course I do! But there's nothing at all I can tell you that will be of any help." He glared at Carol and Bourke over the glossy expanse of his desk. "Besides, I consider that my father's death may well have been a mercy killing."

"What brought you to that conclusion, Mr. Cardover?"

Carol's polite question irritated him. "Well, it's your job to find out, isn't it? Did you check the hospital staff? I've heard of nurses deliberately ending patients' lives. It can't be that rare, can it? My father

117

may have been a victim of some misguided person who thought to relieve his suffering."

"Do you have any firm reason to suspect it was a mercy killing?"

He slapped his hands down on the desk. Leaning forward he said emphatically, "It wasn't murder. That's impossible. And I don't want my mother dragged through some futile investigation for no reason other than a couple of cops have inflated egos."

Carol didn't respond to the gratuitous insult. Intemperate remarks often led a subject to say too much. "We'll be requiring a formal statement from your mother, too."

"This is a total waste of time. My mother doesn't know any more than I do. In other words, nothing."

Bourke consulted his notebook. "Can you tell us where you were when your father died? Say between four-thirty and six-thirty Friday morning."

"You're saying *I'm* a suspect!"

Bourke said smoothly, "It's a formality, but we have to make these inquiries."

"I was in bed. Alone. Then early, about six, I got up and went for a walk."

"You were at your Balmain house?"

He moved impatiently. "Of course."

"What was the weather like?"

Cardover's face reddened. "I don't know. Cold, a bit wet, I think. I had no reason to remember."

Not only had it been less than a week ago, but Carol couldn't imagine a son forgetting details of the day his father died. She said, "Did someone see you during this period? Did you speak to anyone."

"Oh, this is ridiculous!" His chair creaked as he

leaned back and folded his arms. "I've got nothing more to say."

"We've been told," said Carol, "that you had several confrontations with your father in the weeks before he died."

Cardover unfolded his arms. "Who told you that? Marcie Evans?" The grunt he gave showed his loathing. "That bitch. My father let her get away with murder. She was bloody useless, so I had to fire her. No doubt she's got a grudge against me, so I'd advise you not to pay attention to anything she says."

"Quite a few people," said Bourke, "have confirmed that there was conflict between you and your father."

There was silence while Jonathan Cardover digested this. At last he said, "So we argued. So what?"

Carol said, "We've been advised you were concerned about your position in the firm."

Cardover ran a hand over his hair twice, as though stroking himself calm. In a moderate tone, he said, "It's no secret I'm ambitious. I've worked bloody hard for this company, and I want some of the action at the top. I've earned it."

"But," said Carol, "Walter Banning and your father didn't want to give you any added responsibilities. Isn't that right?"

A sneer lifted his upper lip. "Old men, past their prime. It was just a matter of waiting. I've got plenty of time." He pushed back his cuff and glared at his watch, as if it had done something wrong. "I have an urgent appointment, so I'm afraid that's it, Inspector."

"It's possible your father received threats from an environmental organization called Gaia's Revenge," said Bourke.

Cardover got to his feet. "Never heard the name, or if I have, I've forgotten it. I don't pay any attention to extremists. Losers, the whole lot of them. Now, you'll have to excuse me."

"Do you recognize the name Gerald Fitch? Or Bonnie d'Arlene?" said Carol.

Cardover answered almost before she had finished speaking. "Don't know them."

Outside, Bourke said, "When you look at both deaths and ask who gains from them, Jonathan Cardover does, in a big way."

"So does Gaia's Revenge."

"Carol, what's your opinion of this mythical assassin Phoebe Yarmelle mentioned?"

"I hope it's a myth. Fitch isn't above inventing the story to impress someone like Phoebe, especially if he fancies her."

"Fancies her?" said Bourke, shaking his head. "It takes all types."

Back in her office, Carol called Gerald Fitch. He seemed delighted to hear from her. "Inspector! What can I do for you?"

"I have a few questions. I believe Bonnie d'Arlene is visiting. Is that correct?"

"She is here, but I'm afraid you can't meet her. She's off somewhere in the outback. Northern Territory, perhaps, I really can't say. Her plans are elastic, but I know she wants to see some of the beautiful natural places of Australia."

"Will she be in contact with you before she leaves?"

"I imagine so, Inspector. Would you like me to ask Bonnie to call you?"

He sounded eager to please, but Carol smiled ironically, having no expectation that Fitch would follow through with this offer, or any other. She said, "That would be helpful. Now, how about your membership lists? You did say you'd make them available to us."

"Sorry, I haven't got around to collating the names yet," he said airily.

Carol glanced at the folder that held the pages of names Phoebe Yarmelle had provided. "When you can, I'd appreciate it," she said amiably.

"Is that all?" Fitch's tone was helpful. "You know you have my full cooperation."

"We've been speaking to Phoebe Yarmelle," Carol said. "She has given us certain disturbing information."

Fitch laughed. "Let me guess. About a hired killer? Phoebe has an overactive imagination, and I'm afraid we teased her a little, telling her a tall story. I thought she realized she'd been had."

"Apparently not," said Carol. "Ms. Yarmelle seemed convinced that Walter Banning had been the victim of a hit man associated with Gaia's Revenge."

"It's embarrassing that our little joke was taken so seriously."

"Yes, it is, isn't it?" said Carol.

She rang off, convinced that only face to face would she get anywhere with Fitch, who seemed to be enjoying himself far too much for someone who was a possible suspect in a murder.

Eleanor called to arrange for Carol to come to dinner on Friday to discuss David's court appearance, which had been scheduled for the coming week. Carol had squeezed in a quick conversation with her son every day. His cockiness had vanished, and from the questions he asked her it was apparent that he was worried about the children's court and what might happen to him there.

Carol sighed. There seemed no way she could put off plowing through the paperwork that covered her desk. Sitting on top of the pile in her in-box was Sam Goolwa's report on Bonnie d'Arlene. The elusive leader of Gaia had had numerous arrests in the States, all minor infractions related to demonstrations against individuals or institutions perceived by her as threatening the environment, but there was very little else.

Several photographs from a New York arrest had been scanned and transmitted through the Internet. In the full frontal pose, Bonnie d'Arlene glared a challenge at the camera, chin high, her mouth a firm slash. The profile shot showed a strong, hooked nose and a heavy plait down her back.

Carol played with her black opal ring as she locked gazes with the front-face photograph. Bonnie d'Arlene looked both angry and formidable. But a killer?

She called in Anne Newsome and handed her the photographs. "Take a look at Bonnie d'Arlene. She's legally in the country, but no one seems to know where. Don't bother asking Gerald Fitch; he says vaguely she's gone to the outback. She's almost certainly using travelers' checks and credit cards. Find her."

CHAPTER TWELVE

The arrangement was that Carol meet Loren Reece in the hotel lobby at seven-thirty. The dinner booking was for eight at a restaurant famed for its stunning view of Circular Quay and the soaring, flood-lit roofs of the Opera House. Carol had plenty of paperwork to occupy her, so she sent Bourke off with Anne to question Felicity Banning about the divorce she'd neglected to mention, as well as the acrimonious visit she'd paid to her husband's lover.

Carol could have gone straight from work to the hotel, but instead she went home to shower and change, and to feed the feline demands of Sinker, who glared at her malevolently when he realized she was going out again.

She found herself taking special care with her appearance, and chided herself that this was a business date, not a personal one. Nevertheless, she checked herself carefully in a full-length mirror before she left the house. Her blond hair had been recently styled to fall in sleek lines, her emerald earrings enhanced her green eyes, and her dusky rose dress, one of her favorite outfits, was cut on the bias so that the skirt flowed as she moved.

Driving back into the city, Carol thought about the parameters she'd establish with the journalist. There was no way Carol would allow her to be present for interviews of witnesses or suspects. She could, however, observe the running of the office and sit in on briefing sessions, but only with the understanding that she repeat nothing she learned unless it had been cleared with Carol.

Carol wished she'd had the chance to read some of Loren's recent articles. When the journalist was covering a specific person's work, Carol suspected there would still be a strong emphasis on the personal life of the subject. Well, Loren was out of luck if she thought she'd get anything there. Carol had no intention of letting the woman pry into her private life.

Loren was waiting in the Ritz-Carlton lobby when Carol walked in. "You look sensational," she said, smiling.

"You're not so bad yourself." Carol's tone was dry, but she had to acknowledge that Loren Reece, in black as she had been at the gallery, was all understated elegance.

"Shall we walk? I don't believe it's far."

The night was unusually mild, so Carol readily agreed. They strolled down to Circular Quay, which was alive with light and activity. People were streaming along the eastern edge of the cove, obviously for a performance at the Opera House. Passenger ferries busied themselves docking and undocking at the row of wharves that lined the entrance to the city. Carol could hear the soft slap of the tide against the pilings and the mingled smells of oil, tar and salt water tickled her nose.

"Quite a bridge," said Loren, pointing at the huge gray framework that linked the northern and southern shores of the harbor. Faintly, they could hear the roar of the train and see its lights as it paced the traffic on the suspended roadway.

The restaurant looked as expensive as it was. The lights were low, displaying the harbor and city to the best advantage. Loren had organized a table next to the long window, so they looked down on the bustle at the Quay from a new perspective. The attentive waiter, a young man with an extraordinarily handsome face but a soft, spongy body, handed Carol the wine list when Loren asked her to select an Australian vintage.

"Let's not talk business yet," said Loren. "Tell me about Sydney."

"You've been here before, even written an article or two about it," said Carol, "so I doubt I can tell you anything new."

"But it's your city. You know it in a way I never can."

That was true. Carol had lived in Sydney most of her life. She loved it with a clear eye, knowing its astonishing beauty, as well as its mean streets and blighted areas. It was a city blessed with one of the most beautiful harbors in the world, a coastline of glorious surfing beaches, and a mild climate. Whenever she'd been away for any length of time, coming back to it always caused her heart to rise with the delight of returning to her true home.

Carol talked about Sydney and Loren contributed her impressions of other cities around the world as they sipped wine and ate a delicious meal. Over coffee, Loren said with regret, "Perhaps we'd better do some work."

"No tape recorder?"

"I'll use my photographic memory. I doubt if I'll forget anything about you, anyway."

There was a teasing, almost flirtatious note to her voice. Carol had noted on the information Bourke had gathered that Loren had never married. Her speculation must have shown, because Loren grinned and said, "Yes, I am. Let's clear the air. You're quite open about your sexual orientation, I know that. Myself, I don't broadcast it, but I've never denied it if someone asks."

"Before you congratulate me," said Carol sardonically, "I didn't leap out of the closet with enthusiasm. It's hardly an advantage when you're a cop."

"You were married."

"Yes, and divorced. This information isn't relevant to my job."

"Merely background," said Loren. "You have a son."

Carol was instantly wary. "I'm not going to discuss anything about him."

"I've seen a photo. He looks so much like you there was no mistaking he was yours."

"My private life's off limits." Carol was determined to be cool, but she couldn't keep the indignation from her voice. "How in hell did you get a photo of David?"

Loren seemed surprised at Carol's reaction. "No nefarious way, I assure you. It was in a police publicity file. You and David were at a charity sports day to raise money for street kids."

Carol remembered the shot. The photographer had sent her a print, and she had had it framed because it was such a great likeness of David. She and her son had been laughing, arms around each other. He'd needed a haircut, and his knee had been bloody where he'd fallen in the three-legged race, but it was still one of her favorite photographs of him.

"Sorry. I overreacted," she said to make amends.

"You'd better get ready to react again," said Loren. "I'm about to ask you about David being expelled from his school." She grinned at Carol's stony expression. "I'm a journalist, remember? I find out things."

"Since I won't comment to homegrown reporters," said Carol, "I can't imagine why you think I'll talk to you on the subject." She was close to genuine anger now, feeling as if she'd been lulled into false security by the dinner and the relaxed conversation.

Loren leaned over to touch her hand. "Okay, your son's off limits."

The touch had been light, but Carol could still feel her fingers. *Not a chance*, she admonished herself, acknowledging a flicker of desire. It was safer to return to business. "I've been thinking about the areas you'll have access to in the office."

"I hope I'll have access to you."

Carol looked at her levelly. There was no mistaking the meaning in Loren's tone. "I trust you're not aiming to seduce me? That would be very unprofessional."

Loren laughed aloud at Carol's mockery. Raising her glass, she saluted Carol. "Whatever it takes," she said. "Whatever it takes."

CHAPTER THIRTEEN

Carol woke even earlier than usual on Thursday morning, and her first thought was of Loren Reece. Ignoring Sinker, who was adept in exploiting any signs of wakefulness and was on the bed demanding appropriate recognition, Carol lay on her back with her hands behind her head and reviewed the evening. It had been much cooler when they had left the restaurant, but instead of getting a cab, they'd walked briskly back to the hotel, on the way discussing the logistics of Loren's involvement in the day-to-day running of Carol's department. Carol had been keenly aware that underneath their conversation was an undercurrent that had nothing to do with mundane arrangements.

Loren had waited with her while Carol's car was brought from the hotel parking lot. When it arrived, Loren had said, "I really enjoyed this evening," brushed her cheek against Carol's, and gone into the lobby without a backward glance.

"I didn't even rate a sisterly kiss," remarked Carol to Sinker, who had settled his not inconsiderable weight on Carol's chest and was purring loudly in an effort to encourage her to stroke him. As she complied with his demands, she thought, with a touch of discomfort, how much she was looking forward to seeing Loren again today. Carol sat up, dislodging Sinker, who complained testily. It was unwise to read anything more into Loren's manner than mild flirtation. Besides, Carol assured herself, there was no way she was looking for anything more than that herself.

The phone on the bedside table rang. Carol glared at it, but it continued ringing. It was Bourke. "Another one," he said. "Our guy seems to enjoy the thrill of the early morning kill."

"Who is it?"

"Rad Danvers. Shot in the head."

Bourke didn't need to elaborate. Dr. Rad Danvers had been the catalyst for protests by animal activist groups for years. His private company, Danvers & Associates, carried out research mainly on primates on behalf of various chemical and drug companies.

The recent publication of graphic photographs of chimps and other apes undergoing harrowing medical experiments had led to an outcry, but Danvers had brushed aside any criticism, appearing on the media to read a prepared statement: "There is no way that Danvers and Associates will suspend or curtail animal experimentation. Primates are merely animals. Those who try to attribute to them human thoughts and emotions are not only misinformed, but they are also standing in the way of desperately needed medical advances."

Carol scribbled down the address, then rushed to shower and dress. She dumped dry food in Sinker's bowl, checked his water, and hurried out the front door, avoiding building materials and tools as she went. She turned around to survey the mess. For a moment she wondered if her house would ever be completed. Perhaps it would stay in this half-finished state forever. She'd planned to wait and have a stern talk to the builder that morning, but she was leaving so early that even the first workers hadn't arrived.

Bourke met her in front of the anonymous gray building Danvers & Associates owned in the inner suburb of Ultimo. There was no sign to indicate who occupied the premises, only the street number. All the windows were barred, and visitors had to wait for the double metal doors at the entrance to be opened from inside.

"How do the staff get in?" asked Carol.

"Side door down the alley."

Carol went to inspect it, noting that the area had floodlights installed too high for anyone to reach them without a ladder. The door itself was also metal, and it had to be opened with a key and a combination lock together.

"Inside," said Bourke. "It's weird what's happened."

The building was already full of crime-scene technicians. Carol followed Bourke along a corridor to an open door at the end. The smell hit her before she was halfway down. Bourke grinned at her wrinkled nose. "It's the animals. Cages and cages of them."

When they reached the door he stepped aside to give her a clear look. Without protective footwear and gloves, she couldn't enter the direct area of the crime before it had been fully examined. There were no windows. She could hear the muted hum of air-conditioning. Two walls of the room were lined with large, wire-mesh cages. The other walls held rows of glass-fronted cabinets above long benches. The body of a man wearing a white lab coat was lying face down on the dull brown tiles. There was blood at the base of his balding skull. It seemed he'd made no effort to break his fall, as his arms lay slackly beside his body, palms up. The toes of his shoes were turned in, and Carol could see how he'd worn the heels down on the outside edges.

"Dr. Rad Danvers," said Bourke. "Head shot killed him instantly."

"You said something was weird."

"Look in the cages, Carol. Monkeys, apes, whatever. They've been shot. Every one of them is dead."

There was a muffled exclamation behind them. "This is a tragedy! Years of work destroyed!"

The speaker was a narrow-shouldered man with a hatchet face and lank brown hair plastered to his head as though glued in place. He plucked at Carol's arm with slender white fingers. "Are you in charge? You have to find who's done this dreadful thing."

"Ron Fyfield," said Bourke, introducing him. "Mr. Fyfield is Dr. Danvers's assistant."

"Killing those animals!" Fyfield touched Carol's arm again. "Do you have any idea how much vital research has gone down the drain?"

Carol fought the impulse to tell the man to keep his hands to himself. "Is there somewhere we could talk?"

Fyfield waved vaguely in the direction of the front of the building. "My office?"

"Fine. You lead the way."

Fyfield turned and began to hurry down the corridor, dodging crime-scene personnel. Looking past his skinny figure, Carol was surprised to see Loren Reece in jeans and a blue sweater, walking confidently toward them. When she reached Carol, the journalist spoke before Carol could ask her what she was doing in the building. "I've cleared it with Superintendent Edgar, Carol. He says I can sit in as long as I don't get in the way."

This was a battle Carol was going to fight later. She gave Loren a curt nod and went after Fyfield, who was disappearing around a corner up ahead. Bourke and Loren followed her. She could hear them talking behind her, Loren saying something about getting into the office very early to take some Polaroid photos for later reference, and finding that Rad Danvers had been murdered and that Carol was on the case.

Ron Fyfield was already safely seated behind a dented metal desk in an untidy room stacked with folders, files and loose papers. A computer monitor and keyboard took up most of the desk's surface, the rest of the area being crowded with dirty coffee mugs, paper plates that had once held what looked like Chinese food, and several plastic foam cups.

He held the telephone receiver in one hand as he checked through an ancient card file with the other. "I have to tell everybody," he said in explanation. "God knows what will happen now." His gaunt face was lit with a sudden idea. "Perhaps autopsies of the animals can give us some information. There may be something we can salvage."

He looked at Carol, Loren and Bourke in turn, as though expecting them to make noises of approval. Carol leaned over, took the receiver from him, and replaced it on the phone set. "I know you're anxious to advise people, Mr. Fyfield, but it's very important we have all the relevant information from you first."

"There's nothing to tell. I came in early to run an experiment and found Rad lying on the floor and all the animals in that area killed."

"When did you last see Dr. Danvers alive?"

"Last night. He was working late and told me to go home. I was the last person to leave, around eight I think, so Rad was all alone in the building. That wasn't unusual — he always said he did his best work after midnight. There's a sofa bed in his office, so he often sleeps here."

A sly smile crossed his face. "Actually, I got the idea that Rad was expecting someone. He practically pushed me out of the building."

"Do you have any idea who the person might be?"

Fyfield snickered a little. "Not a clue, but she'd be pretty rough, I'd reckon. Everyone here knew Rad would bring women back here from time to time. He shares a house with his old mother, and that cramps his style at home."

Carol noticed that Loren had positioned herself obtrusively in on a plastic chair and had an open notebook on her knees. Loren caught her glance and gave her a slight smile. Carol looked away.

Bourke said, "Please go through what happened this morning."

Fyfield looked at the ceiling for inspiration, then said, "Okay, it went down like this. I got here at five-thirty on the dot. I like to start early before the staff arrive and the phones start ringing. Best time of day to get things done. I keyed in the code at the side door — it changes every week — came here to my office to drop off my things, then went straight down to Lab Four, where I found someone had slaughtered the chimps."

Fyfield pursed his lips, obviously scandalized. "What kind of person would commit such willful destruction? Those research animals were irreplaceable. Irreplaceable!"

"Dr. Danvers was also killed," Bourke observed.

"That, of course, is a catastrophe." Fyfield's tone was matter-of-fact. "But the work can go on without him."

Carol asked, "Could the murder have anything to do with your company's current research projects?"

Fyfield pulled his head back, as though he wore an invisible shell and could hide himself in it. "I'm not at liberty to discuss our clients' business."

Noting how the man appeared to be much more upset about the death of the animals than the murder of his superior, Carol said, "What sort of working relationship did you have with Dr. Danvers?"

"Working relationship?" Fyfield looked at her with suspicion. "An excellent one, of course."

"Rad Danvers got a lot of media attention."

Fyfield gave Carol a thin smile. "If you're asking did I resent the fact the focus was on him? Not at all. He had to deal with all those pathetic protesters." He made a slashing motion across his throat. "Jesus, I'm up to here with the bleeding hearts. They'd be the first to scream for a new drug, whether it was tested on a chimp or not, but in the meantime they make our lives miserable with their stupid demonstrations."

In the silence that followed this remark, Carol could hear Loren flip over a page in her notebook.

"Have you or Dr. Danvers received any specific threats lately?"

A lift of narrow shoulders. "No more than usual."

An officer in uniform came to the door and beckoned to Bourke. After a short conversation, Bourke came back into the room to say, "Some of those bleeding hearts are demonstrating outside right now."

"The media here yet?" asked Carol.

"Yep. Causing quite a traffic jam." Bourke said to Fyfield, "Does the name *Gaia's Revenge* seem familiar to you?"

He shook his head emphatically. "I don't waste time remembering the ridiculous names they give themselves."

"How about Gerald Fitch or Bonnie d'Arlene?"

A frown creased his pale forehead. "That last one? What was the name again?" He nodded slowly. "Yeah, I know her. A Yank. She was here in the building last week, talking with Rad. And don't ask me what about, because I don't know."

Carol left Bourke questioning Fyfield, motioning Loren to follow her outside into the corridor. "I can't have you in the room while I'm dealing with witnesses."

"I'm not listening to the interview. I'm there for background on how you work and how you handle people."

Carol sighed with exasperation. "You were taking notes."

"Nothing to do with what Fyfield was saying. I was jotting down details of how you looked, the way you talked. I want readers to see you as a real person, not just as a cop."

"None of this is a good idea."

Abruptly, Loren seemed impatient. "I'm just doing my job. Your superiors say to me, fine, okay, go ahead. Why can't you?"

"Because you're intruding on an investigation."

"I'm not, and you know I'm not."

Bourke put his head out the door. "Fyfield's just told me Bonnie d'Arlene and Rad Danvers seemed quite chummy together. Don't you find that remarkable?"

"I've asked Anne to find the woman. As soon as she's located, we can ask her why she was on such good terms with such an arch enemy of Gaia."

Leaving Bourke in charge of the crime scene, Carol decided to go back to headquarters. "Are you going to dog me everywhere?" she snapped at Loren when the journalist followed her.

"Everywhere," said Loren, imperturbable.

Outside the weather was bleak. It had begun to rain, a cold, heavy shower that was driven into their faces by a stiff breeze. The inclement conditions had thinned the crowd outside the building, but a few hardy people remained, most of them holding wet signs supporting animal rights. One teenage girl waved a placard declaring, TORTURE ALL THE TORTURERS!

Drenched TV crews in yellow slickers focused on the protesters while waiting for something more exciting to occur. As soon as Carol came out of the front doors the television cameras turned her way. Loren put up an umbrella to shield herself, but Carol ignored the rain and hurried toward her car, scanning the meager crowd to see if she recognized anyone. Almost immediately she saw Gerald Fitch, who acknowledged her with a cheerful wave. A reporter thrust a microphone in front of her, and Carol murmured, "No comment at this time." Then she was in the shelter of her vehicle.

Rain was thrumming on the roof and streaming down the glass in front of her. Carol peered around to see what had happened to Loren, but she had disappeared.

Anne Newsome met Carol as Carol came out of the restroom where she'd been brushing her hair dry. "You'll never guess who's waiting to see you!"

Feeling damp and irritable, Carol said, "Unless it's someone to tell me I've won the lottery, I'm not interested."

"No lottery," Anne said, "but you know you told me to find Bonnie d'Arlene? Before I could trace her, she'd come in herself. She's sitting in your office right now."

"She just turned up?"

"Appeared at the front desk announcing that she needed to see Inspector Ashton urgently." Anne gave a mock frown. "I tried to ask her a few questions, but she's holding out for you."

"Sit in on the interview, Anne. This is going to be interesting."

The woman who rose to greet Carol was, not surprisingly, better looking than her mug shots had indicated. Her long brown hair was in one plait that she had draped over her left shoulder. Her face with its hooked nose, so uncompromisingly grim in the shots taken after her arrest, was softened by a winning smile. "Inspector Ashton, I'm delighted to meet you."

Bonnie d'Arlene was in slacks and boots. Her pale pink cashmere top was expensive, as were the pearl earrings she wore.

"I don't look like your average eco-freak do I?" she asked, obviously amused at Carol's measuring glance. "Perhaps you were expecting shorts and an unironed shirt made of natural fibers?"

Carol grinned. "I do hate it when my preconceptions are shattered," she said, finding that she liked the woman at first sight. On guard because of this, she withdrew into her official, cool self. "It's very convenient that you've made yourself available, Ms.

d'Arlene, as we do have some questions about the activities of your organization."

"Please call me Bonnie, Inspector. Everyone does. As to the organization, it isn't mine. It belongs to all those who want a better world for our children." She gave a little gurgle of laughter. "There, I've got the soapbox stuff over, so we can get down to business."

Carol glanced over to Anne, who had opened her notebook and was ready to record any items of interest. Carol said, "I believe you were in the Danvers and Associates' building last week."

"I was," Bonnie said agreeably. "I was talking with that monster, Rad Danvers."

"A monster who has been murdered in the last few hours."

Bonnie nodded agreement with Carol's blunt statement. "An excellent outcome."

"Why were you meeting with him?"

Bonnie d'Arlene's expression became bleak. "Sometimes you have to negotiate with the devil, Inspector. I was there to discuss limiting the animal trials Danvers was conducting. I was pushing the many alternatives that now exist. It seems to me that it's sheer laziness and fear of advanced technology that keeps these people doing things the old way, and Danvers was a Luddite from way back. And his assistant, Fyfield, was worse, if that's possible. A nasty little man with no redeeming features whatsoever."

"So you didn't get anywhere with Dr. Danvers?"

"On the contrary, Inspector, he listened when I showed him the figures. It's not cost effective to use animals when there are better ways. He may have been an unprincipled brute, but Rad Danvers could never be accused of being financially illiterate." She grinned at Carol's carefully neutral expression. "Believe it or not, I do prefer soft persuasion if it'll work. Unfortunately it rarely does, so we have to use more direct means."

Carol said, "Would you tell me where you were from eight last night to until five-thirty this morning?"

"I was staying with Gerald Fitch at his house."

"Mr. Fitch said that you were touring remote areas of Australia."

"Don't chastise Gerald for lying, Inspector. I asked him to keep my whereabouts deliberately vague." With another charming smile, she added, "Frankly, I don't welcome media attention unless I can manipulate it for the good of Gaia's Revenge. I'm sure that you, with your high media profile, would understand that."

Don't try to manipulate me, Carol thought. Aloud she said, "So you were in the company of Mr. Fitch for that entire period?"

"We are each other's alibi," Bonnie said, clearly amused. "Perhaps it looks a little suspicious, but I assure you we were together until breakfast, when we heard the news flash about the death of Dr. Danvers. We realized that there'd be television cameras, so Gerald immediately organized a protest group and left. I finished a leisurely breakfast, and, knowing you would almost certainly want to see me, I saved you the trouble of a search by coming here myself."

"That was very helpful of you," said Carol.

Bonnie d'Arlene sat back in her chair. "Fire away, Inspector. I've got nothing to hide."

It had been Carol's experience that interviewees

who announced they had nothing to hide almost always did. She said, "How would you know I'd be on this particular case?"

"Oh, Inspector," chided Bonnie, "it's perfectly obvious there's a pattern of murders here. Of course you'd be the detective in charge of this investigation."

CHAPTER FOURTEEN

"What did you make of her, Anne?" Carol asked after the interview had concluded and Bonnie d'Arlene had been escorted out by a junior officer.

"She seems pleasant enough, but that doesn't mean much." Anne flicked the pages of her notebook. "How is it that both Bonnie d'Arlene and Fitch seem to be going out of their way to set themselves up as suspects? Just for the publicity?"

"Or to deflect attention from someone else. What's happening with the membership lists Phoebe Yarmelle handed over?"

"Miles is cross-checking the names, but no one's leapt out as a serial killer," said Anne. Grinning, she added, "If you ask me, both Bonnie d'Arlene and Gerald Fitch are rabid enough to kill for what they believe in, so they get my vote as Bonnie and Fitch Murder Incorporated."

Carol considered Anne's flippant remark. "It might seem bizarre on the surface," she said, "but these are two people totally united in a common cause and, if we are to believe what they say, convinced that murder is quite a reasonable strategy to protect the natural world."

Anne nodded soberly. "Even in my animal rights group, there are members who want to go to extremes. When you see what's unthinkingly done to living things in the name of science or worse, commercial product testing, violence somehow seems almost like justice."

"I want a check on the movements of both d'Arlene and Fitch for the time frames of all the murders."

"Edward Guthrie, too?"

Carol had disregarded Guthrie's death after all reports had indicated it had been a hunting accident, but now she wondered if she'd been too hasty. "Edward Guthrie, too. The local cops confirmed that Fitch was attending a retreat in the Blue Mountains when Guthrie was shot, but he could have slipped out unseen. As for Bonnie d'Arlene, she'd just arrived from the States. Check the Bondi hotel she gave as her initial address."

Anne started to stand, but Carol motioned her to stay. "What happened when you and Mark saw Felicity Banning yesterday?"

Anne made a face. "She cried a lot. Got almost hysterical."

Carol visualized the exhausted woman she'd seen on Sunday. Banning's wife had seemed numbed by grief.

"Hysterical? Why?"

"When we asked how it was she hadn't heard the gunshots, since the garage is right under the kitchen, she admitted that over breakfast she'd had a no-holds-barred fight with her husband. He walked out, slamming the door behind him, and she says she was so upset she ran sobbing into the bedroom at the back of the house and stayed there for at least half an hour."

"She couldn't hear two gunshots through her tears?" said Carol, skeptical.

"So it seems."

"And Phoebe Yarmelle?"

"She claimed not to know the name, but when Mark read part of Phoebe's statement, Felicity Banning broke down again." Anne shook her head. "It made me feel like a bit of a brute, asking her questions while she was crying."

"Maybe that's what she wanted you to feel."

Anne acknowledged Carol's tart comment with a quick grin. "Could be."

"She admitted confronting Phoebe, did she?"

"Eventually she said that she was desperate to save her marriage, so she went to plead with her husband's girlfriend on more than one occasion, begging her not to continue the affair."

Carol couldn't imagine any circumstances that could drive her to the point of imploring a rival to stop seeing someone Carol loved.

"Had Banning taken any steps to initiate divorce proceedings?" Carol asked.

"She said not, but Mark's checking to see if that's true." Anne stood up, jigging a little as though impatient to be off and doing something positive. "All this is just a waste of time if Walter Banning's death was a hit. Now that Danvers has been murdered too, isn't it pretty obvious that Banning was an outside job?"

Carol smiled at her constable. "You're just keen to have an environmentally sound serial killer out there, aren't you?"

"It'd be different," said Anne.

Carol saw Loren talking to Anne and Miles Li, but the journalist didn't come near Carol's office. Bourke reported in as soon as he returned from the Ultimo crime scene. "The preliminary time of death is late evening to early morning. The animals were killed about the same time."

"They were all shot?"

"Every one of them. Fyfield says they were infected with virulent diseases." His mouth turned down. "Poor things, it's obvious they were suffering a lot, so someone put them out of their misery."

"We may get lucky with ballistics. There were a lot of rounds fired in that room."

"Tell me," said Bourke. "Whoever it was had to reload at least once."

Knowing the answer before she asked, Carol said, "No sign of forced entry?"

"None, so if it isn't an inside job, someone let the

murderer into the building. I've asked around, but no one else had any inkling Danvers was intending to entertain female company that night."

"If he was. We only have Fyfield's word on that. Does he have a motive?"

"Hey, Carol, almost anyone who worked with or for Rad Danvers had good reasons to eliminate him. I gather he was not only unpleasant as a person, but he also routinely took credit for colleagues' work, belittled their achievements, and generally behaved like a total fuckwit. Plus there're rumors he was cooking his lab results so he could report to his clients what they wanted to hear."

"Bonnie d'Arlene turned up here of her own free will because she thought I'd like to question her," said Carol with an ironic smile. "I thanked her for being so helpful. She was pleased to tell me how she spent valuable time with Danvers, successfully persuading him to reduce animal trials in the future."

Bourke looked doubtful. "Do you believe her?"

"It's possible, but unlikely. Danvers doesn't seem the sort to even give the time of day to someone who represents the very groups he's attacked so viciously in the past."

"Fyfield said that Danvers and Bonnie d'Arlene talked for some time with no fireworks," said Bourke. "Maybe she was lulling Danvers into a sense of false security before she blew him away."

"Could be. The woman's certainly got the motivation, and, I suspect, the guts to carry it out. She claims to have spent all the time from dinner last night to breakfast this morning in the company of Gerald Fitch."

When Bourke raised his eyebrows, she added, "I

hate to dash your hopes, but I doubt they're sexual partners, Mark. She's staying with him while she goes about Gaia's business."

"You never know," said Bourke.

"You don't," said Carol. Perhaps she'd missed something. Colleagues who were also lovers had a strengthened bond of loyalty, and were likely to lie for each other without hesitation.

"I'd like to see Fitch here, out of his usual territory," said Carol.

Bourke got up. "Right. He was still in a demo when I left Ultimo, but the TV crews were packing up, so I reckon he'd head for shelter, either at the office or in the nearest coffee shop. I'll send Sam Goolwa after him."

She spent an hour going through her mail. As promised, Phoebe Yarmelle's anonymous letter was there, carefully printed in block capitals. She was smiling at its earnest tone when Miles Li knocked at the door. Bourke was with him.

"Those Gaia membership lists Anne asked me to cross-check," Li said. "You might be interested in one name that's come up."

"Who?"

"Phoebe Yarmelle."

Putting down the letter, Carol gave Li her full attention. "What about her?"

"You know how she was supposed to join the Gaia group just to please Banning? Well, she's an activist from way back, but under a different name. She changed her name legally by deed poll two years ago, but the computer picked her up because of a match on place and date of birth. I checked her out and found a pretty impressive arrest record."

"These environmentalists are just falling out of the trees," said Bourke.

Li passed Carol a printout. "Phoebe Watts she was then. Chained herself to trees, lay down in front of logging machines, the whole saving-the-trees bit. Then she was involved in a pretty spectacular stunt when a group protesting cruel conditions in abattoirs dumped liters of blood all over the steps of government house as well as a few pollies that got in the way. She was arrested for that, got a stiff fine and hours of community service. Then she changed her name and pretty well disappeared."

"One might ask," said Bourke, "why someone with Phoebe's background would start an affair with a notorious polluter like Walter Banning."

"Ask," said Carol to Bourke. "And find out where she was when Rad Danvers was killed."

"Care to go sailing with me?"

Carol looked up from the report she was reading. "Sailing?"

Loren grinned at her. "Don't look at me like that. It's an entirely genuine offer. A journalist friend — well, more an acquaintance — has a little yacht he's offered to let me borrow this coming weekend. How about it?"

Indicating her overburdened desk, Carol said, "Thanks for the invitation, but I have to make some headway here. I haven't time to spare."

"Sure you have. Just a couple of hours on Saturday afternoon. I'll even let you come back to work afterward, if you insist."

It was tempting. Carol loved the water. And she had to admit that Loren Reece's company held a certain temptation too. "Are you a good sailor?" she asked.

"Good? I'm terrific. I grew up in San Diego, California, and I could sail a boat almost before I could walk." She spread her hands. "Well?"

"All right, for a couple of hours," said Carol, knowing that she was capitulating without even the pretense of a struggle.

"You've got it," said Loren. "Now, how about dinner tonight?"

That was a definite no. Carol was taking home everything that had come in on the membership of Gaia's Revenge, plus the preliminary postmortem on Danvers, which the pathologist had been persuaded to do immediately. "Sorry, Loren. Rain check?"

"Sunday night, then, and I won't be put off." Loren slid gracefully onto the chair by Carol's desk. "I hope you notice how I haven't been getting in your way," she said virtuously. She put an elbow on a pile of papers and rested her chin on her hand. "So the least you can do is fill me in with what's happening."

"Why do you need specific details? I thought the article was about me," Carol said lightly.

"It is about you, but not in the static sense." She laughed, then continued. "I'm portraying you in action, chasing after your quarry like a well-bred hound." Her smile faded as she went on. "Seriously, Carol, these murders are part of a pattern, aren't they? It's fascinating to me to see the ins and outs of your investigation. I'm convinced the story I write will be Pulitzer Prize material."

"I imagine you can get the necessary background from others," said Carol. "You were talking with Anne Newsome, for example."

"She admires you very much."

"Oh, spare me!" said Carol. "Sweet-talking will get you nowhere." She grabbed her briefcase and began stuffing papers into it.

"I believe I've been dismissed," said Loren without any sign that she was offended. Carol watched her walk out of the room. At the door she looked back over her shoulder with a smile, then she was gone.

It was irritating, thought Carol, that there was something addictive about Loren's company. It would have been easy to say yes to dinner tonight. Too easy.

When Carol arrived home she found the builder had left an envelope containing the details of a progress payment that he claimed was due. "You'll be lucky to get it," she said aloud, looking around at the shambles of what would eventually be her new living room. Tomorrow she'd waylay the man and get a firm finishing date from him. He was using the excuse of the unusual number of rainy days for the delay in completion, and Carol knew there was substance in his excuse, but nevertheless she was ready to be militant when she faced him.

Sinker followed her into the kitchen, which was starting to look almost complete, although everything was covered with a layer of fine dust and the tiles were gritty under her feet. She felt too tired to go to any trouble, so she scrambled eggs, made toast, cleared a space on the bench, and perched on a kitchen stool to watch Madeline's show on the television set wedged precariously next to the stove.

The Shipley Report appeared on the screen in red, followed by a closeup of Madeline's attractive face. "A pattern of environmental assassinations!" she exclaimed. "Are these mysterious deaths linked in some shocking way?" A shot of Fitch, looking suitably grave, appeared. Sam Goolwa had located him late that afternoon, and Fitch had promised to be in Carol's office first thing Friday. On the screen, Madeline declared, "Gerald Fitch, the man who can answer the question: Is there a serial killer loose in Sydney?"

Carol groaned to herself. She'd fielded calls from journalists all afternoon, and on the way home she'd listened to the news on the car radio, not surprised to find the speculation about a link between the deaths of Banning, Cardover and Danvers was a hot topic. Now with Madeline's dramatic approach, an official media statement tomorrow was inevitable.

The Shipley Report was highly regarded as a newsmagazine, but this time Madeline had gone for sensational accusations, unsupported by facts. She did limit Fitch's attempts to publicize Gaia's Revenge, putting the focus squarely on the deaths that might be motivated by the victims' destruction of the environment. Carol was interested to see that Madeline had included Edward Guthrie, as well as a couple of the overseas names from Gaia's Web site.

The segment had just concluded when the phone rang. Superintendent Edgar's voice boomed down the line. "Carol? You've been watching the Shipley woman's program? I've got PR to set up a media conference for you tomorrow morning. Make sure you're up to speed, okay? And see me first thing. We want to come across as being on top of this."

With a cynical smile, she put down the handset. Edgar had obviously decided that the pleasure he'd gain being the center of media attention wasn't worth the risk of making a fool of himself.

CHAPTER FIFTEEN

Friday started with a perfect morning. The rain had gone and the sky was clear. Carol ran through bushland washed clean and full of delicious wet scents, accompanied by an excited Olga, who had missed her outing the day before. Carol returned home to find the builder waiting for her. "Good news," he said. "I've moving some of my guys from another site so we can finish up here quick smart. Bet that'll please you, Carol."

"What's quick smart?" said Carol, ever suspicious of Kev, as he insisted on being called.

"Four weeks, tops," Kev declared. "That is, if it doesn't rain again."

"I see you left a bill for a progress payment," said Carol, with the thought that Kev's show of enthusiasm for finishing the job might be related to securing this substantial sum.

He beamed at her. "Want to settle it now?"

"I'll mail it," said Carol.

"That cat of yours is a terror," said Kev, observing Sinker clambering over timber that had just been delivered. He grinned at Carol. "Nearly lost his tail in the circular saw yesterday. It was a near thing, I can tell you."

"You hurt my cat," said Carol grinning in turn, "and you'll get no progress payment from me."

She was still in a good humor when she arrived at work. To have her house finished and livable again was something to look forward to with joy. Next time, if there ever was a next time, she promised herself she'd move out while the alterations were done, no matter how much extra it cost.

She greeted Bourke with a smile. "How's Carli?"

Usually he could be depended upon to describe his daughter's latest achievements in exhaustive detail, but this morning he dismissed the subject with, "She's fine."

"Something bothering you?"

"It'll bother you, too. Phoebe Yarmelle, or Watts, if you prefer, has skipped. No trace of her anywhere. When I couldn't get her yesterday, I assumed she was out somewhere, but I went over to her place this morning and chatted up her next door neighbor. It seems Phoebe appeared on his doorstep last night with a suitcase in hand and told him she was going away for a few weeks. She didn't say where, just gave him a key and asked him to water her plants and collect her mail."

"Did she leave in her car?"

Bourke shook his head. "No such luck. Her car's still parked under the building. The neighbor didn't see who picked her up. I've got Anne checking the taxi companies, but I think our Phoebe's done a runner, and she's going to be hard to find."

"Alert the federal police. I don't want her flying out of the country."

"Done that," said Bourke. "But even if we locate her, we've got no grounds to arrest her, have we?"

"Not yet," said Carol. "Have we got a photo of her?"

"There's a mug shot dating back to her last arrest as Phoebe Watts. It's a good likeness."

"Get it circulated." Struck with a sudden thought, Carol added, "And check out Bonnie and Fitch, as Anne calls them. Maybe Phoebe's better friends with them than she ever made out."

Superintendent Edgar wasn't pleased. "You let this Phoebe Yarmelle slip through your fingers?"

"We had no reason to suspect that she was guilty of anything other than keeping quiet about her activist past," said Carol, stung by his criticism.

Edgar gave an unhappy grunt. "What if she's the serial killer Madeline Shipley's got everyone stirred up about? What if Yarmelle's put on a great act, and you've fallen for it?"

Carol felt a wave of irritation wash over her. Keeping her voice even, she said, "First, there's no hard evidence that there *is* a serial murderer. Second, her only connection to the case is that she had a relationship with Walter Banning. What's more, we've turned up a lawyer Banning approached to start proceedings for divorce. It seems to me it was to Phoebe Yarmelle's advantage to keep Walter Banning alive."

Even as she said these words, Carol considered whether she really believed them. Phoebe had fooled her, and Bourke, and very possibly Walter and Felicity Banning. The super was right. It could all be a very convincing act.

The media conference was packed. It had been a slow week for news, and the thought of a killer stalking high-profile victims was irresistible to everyone associated with press, radio, or television. Carol noticed Loren off to one side, accompanied by a photographer, and thought sardonically how fortunate it was that she had gone to special trouble with her makeup, knowing that her face would be on the evening news.

The questions came heavy and fast, and Carol parried them with skill. She always felt a little more alive under pressure like this. It was like a high-stakes game, where she was the focus of attack yet armed with expertise that allowed her to prevail. And she was also aware that she had a duty to present facts fairly, but in such a way that the investigation would not be compromised.

Edgar, arms folded, lurked at the back of the

crowd. After twenty minutes he strode into the glare of the lights at the front. "There's no more we can say at this point," he said. "As soon as we have further information, you'll be informed."

"Great stuff," said Loren as Carol maneuvered from behind the long desk. "Could Stan get a few more photographs for the article?"

Complying with good grace, Carol smiled on cue, looked pensive, and gazed thoughtfully at a page Loren handed her as a prop. "You sure you don't want me looking through a large magnifying glass?" she asked.

"A delightful idea," said Loren, chuckling, "but perhaps a little old-fashioned. How about posing you in front of a computer monitor. That's more like it."

Gerald Fitch showed up at eleven-thirty, much later than he had promised. His appearance on television seemed to have puffed up his self-esteem. "Did you see me on *The Shipley Report* last night?" he asked Carol as soon as he was seated. He had on the same crumpled blue suit that he'd been wearing the first time she'd met him. Even his creased shirt and carelessly knotted tie seemed the same.

"I did watch you," said Carol, "and I'm interested to know where you got your information about an international campaign to assassinate those people designated as enemies of the earth."

"Merely conjecture, Inspector. Of course if I had any hard evidence, I'd have contacted you immediately."

"Of course," said Carol. "When did you last see Phoebe Yarmelle?"

"When we threw her out of the organization. Why?"

"You didn't know that her name was originally Phoebe Watts?"

He answered too quickly, "I had no idea she had another name."

"It's strange you should say that," said Carol, referring to a printout of Fitch's record of arrests that Bourke had given her that morning. "It says here that you were arrested two years ago at an incident where blood was poured on the steps of parliament house on Macquarie Street."

He nodded affably. "A very successful demonstration, as I remember."

"Phoebe Watts, as she was called then, was arrested at the same demonstration."

He kept his face blank. "Are you sure? I don't recall that."

Carol passed him Phoebe's mug shot. "Do you recognize her?"

"Yes, this is Phoebe Yarmelle." He shrugged. "There were a lot of people on the steps that day."

Carol leaned back and considered him. Fitch, a half-smile on his face, stared back at her. They both knew he was lying, Carol thought. The intriguing question was why.

"Ms. Yarmelle has disappeared," she said. "Would you know anything about that?"

He lifted his shoulders again. "Search me." With a grin he added, "I'm not concealing her at my house, if that's what you think."

Carol questioned Fitch for another fifteen minutes but extracted no useful information from him. After he'd gone she sat doodling on a notepad while she imagined possible scenarios that would fit the situation.

Reluctantly she had to acknowledge that it was more than likely that there was a serial murderer at work. The slugs taken from Danvers and the chimps matched in weight the twenty-twos taken from Banning, and the modus operandi in the two cases was the same: an assailant efficiently dispatching victims with a shot to the head, entering and leaving the scene without witnesses.

Cardover's death in the hospital, however, was sufficiently different for Carol to leave it in a separate category for the time being, as there was still a possibility that his demise had been accomplished by someone close to him, his son being the best possibility.

Bourke had interviewed Nurse Slade again, and had come back with the firm opinion that because Cardover had had potential for improvement, unlike her two totally comatose patients in Melbourne, it was very unlikely that Marilyn Slade had attempted another mercy killing.

The shooting of Edward Guthrie was also inconclusive, although Carol now had the gut feeling that it was another deliberate assassination.

She wrote down Fitch's name and drew a circle around it. She could imagine him in the role of executioner. She could visualize his mild face hardened by a deadly determination to achieve vengeance. He was not a man who would appear to be a physical threat to anyone, a distinct advantage in getting close to victims. And there was no doubt about Fitch's commitment to environmentalism. He had quite literally devoted his life to active pursuit of individuals and organizations that threatened the integrity of the ecosystem.

Fitch had the opportunity, the motivation, but where was the weapon? She could initiate a search of his home and Gaia's offices, but Carol was convinced that it would be fruitless. The gun, she felt sure, had now been disposed of, and even if it were found, the likelihood that the weapon would provide evidence leading to a suspect was slim.

Bonnie d'Arlene was perhaps an even worthier suspect. Carol had no trouble conjuring up a picture of Bonnie with a gun in her hand, her eyes narrowed with righteous hatred. She'd entered the country before Edward Guthrie had been killed, and any alibis she had for the time of the murders were unreliable. She'd met Rad Danvers before his murder, and had apparently been on good terms with him, so it wasn't a stretch to think that he might freely let her enter the building after hours.

And then there was Phoebe Yarmelle. Carol frowned over the photograph on her desk. Two years ago her hair had been shorter, her face a little thinner, but she had the same wide-eyed intensity that had impressed Carol when she had interviewed her on Wednesday. Without her high heels Phoebe would barely come to Carol's shoulder. No man, surely, would see her as a menacing figure. Carol thought of Walter Banning obligingly opening the window of his Rolls so he could be shot without the inconvenience of shattering glass. If Phoebe had suddenly appeared in his garage he might have been astounded, but not fearful for his life.

Dr. Danvers, too, would never consider someone like Phoebe any danger to his well-being. It wasn't difficult to come up with some stratagem that would get Phoebe into the building and down to the room where Danvers and the caged animals were slaughtered.

On the pad, Carol linked the names with arrows: Gerald Fitch; Bonnie d'Arlene; Phoebe Yarmelle/Watts. She drew a double circle around Phoebe. Was she the key to the puzzle?

Carol couldn't help feeling that the three of them were working together, that somehow they were setting up a situation where each of them became a viable suspect, but with no hard evidence to isolate the real killer.

She threw down her pen with the discouraging thought that maybe each of the three had executed one victim. It was an extraordinary prospect, but Carol could almost believe that it might be true.

Bourke found her in the cramped office kitchen looking doubtfully into a mug of coffee. "I'm scared to taste it," she said to him. "It looks even worse than usual."

"Here's something to really scare you," said Bourke. "Dick Juno is coming to town to complete some business deal. If ever there was a target for an environmentalist activist with a gun, it would be him."

Juno was a Canadian entrepreneur notorious for the damage his mining company had done in several areas, most notably to the Amazon rain forest. The near-extinction of several rare animals had been attributed to his company's activities. He was totally unrepentant about the ravages his mining methods had caused, and never hesitated to use legal action against protesters. It was rumored that he bought and sold local politicians and that he maintained his own personal squad of mercenaries to enforce his will in remote locations.

"He'll have to be warned."

Bourke's mouth quirked. "Pity we have to do it," he said.

CHAPTER SIXTEEN

Carol woke on Saturday morning with a sense of anticipation that surprised her with its intensity. She made a face at herself as she cleaned her teeth. Going sailing with Loren Reece didn't really merit this level of enthusiasm.

Perhaps her lighthearted feeling was related to her son. Last night Carol had sat down to dinner at her ex-husband's house, the first time since their divorce that she had shared a meal with him. She, Justin, Eleanor and David had discussed David's appearance in front of the children's court, which was scheduled for the next Tuesday.

David's former attitude that it all wasn't fair that he'd been charged with anything at all had changed markedly. He'd been subdued, but open in admitting that he realized he'd been stupid and that he could see he deserved to be punished. Carol was pleased that David had come to terms with the gravity of the situation, and also that Justin had obviously become more supportive and less censorious.

"Will you be there, Mum?" David had asked. "I know you're busy on a case."

"Wild horses couldn't keep me away."

David had seen her out to her car. When she hugged him good-bye, he'd said, "Dad says if I never do anything like this again, it'll be wiped off my record, like it never happened. That's true, isn't it?"

"That's true."

David had given her a small grin. "I guarantee I won't be doing anything like this again. Honest."

Carol smiled, thinking of his earnest tone as he had made the promise. She had no doubt that David would be considerably less chastened once his court appearance was over. As a first offender, he'd get a stern talking to and be put on probation. Soon his life would be back to normal. Justin had pulled strings mightily, and David was enrolled in another private school. It was not one that had the social clout of David's former establishment, and it was coeducational, a fact that Justin frowned upon, but basically the school was quite acceptable.

She dressed in jeans and sneakers, and sat down with the contents of her briefcase spread over the heavy wooden table on the deck. The air was warmed by a hint of spring, and the dappled light glancing through the leaves of the surrounding eucalyptus gum trees danced on the papers in front of her. Dick Juno was flying in this weekend, and the commissioner himself was going to brief the magnate about the possible danger. From past performances, Carol was sure that Juno would be scornful of any threat from eco-pimps, as he derisively called them.

At eleven-thirty she packed everything away. As she did so, she advised Sinker to forget stalking the magpies who were building an early nest in one of the overhanging trees, pointing out that any one black-and-white magpie would be more than a match for a black-and-white cat.

The yacht Loren was borrowing was moored at a marina near the Spit Bridge, which spanned the narrowest part of Middle Harbour, so it was only a few minutes away from Carol's house.

Loren greeted her with a smile and a hug. "I've got food, I've got drink, and now I have my own detective inspector."

The yacht was larger than Carol had expected. It could sleep six at a pinch, and it had a well-designed galley and a generous dining area. Loren showed her around, then said, "Let's go!"

Carol was a competent sailor, but she had to acknowledge that Loren's talents were far superior. From the moment Loren cast off and motored *Sea Song* out of the marina, it was clear she knew exactly what she was doing. Once the sails were set and the strong breeze had sent the yacht scudding along, heeling over the flying spray, Loren took charge absolutely. Content to be the crew, Carol obeyed her commands, scrambling to whatever station the skipper required.

"You're a Captain Queeg," Carol said, laughing as she ducked to avoid being decapitated by the boom as they changed direction.

It was a glorious day to be on the water. The wind was cool, not cold, and the water scintillated under a cloudless sky. The huge blue expanse of Sydney Harbour was dotted with yachts of all sizes, from oceangoing beauties to tiny one-person vessels that consisted mainly of a sail and a minute hull.

"Do you know where you're going?" Carol called as they rounded Middle Head and set course for the main part of the harbor.

"Don't worry, I've studied the maps." Loren tacked expertly, sensing the exact moment to come about. They rocked in the wash of a Manly-bound catamaran ferry that was scooting at considerable speed along the surface of the water. "Isn't this great!" Loren shouted above the roar of the ferry's engines.

It was great. Carol couldn't recall feeling so relaxed yet exhilarated. And Loren was vibrant company, her face turned to the sun, her dark hair lashed by the wind, her sailing skills pushing the little yacht to the limit.

"Hungry?"

"Starving," said Carol.

Loren took them back toward Middle Harbour, bringing the yacht about expertly and dropping anchor in a little sheltered cove that was part of Sydney

Harbour National Park. It was like a private piece of heaven. The vegetation came right down to the water, there was a little curve of sandy beach, and no other boats were anywhere near them. A few seagulls bobbed in the water, others squabbled with each other on the tumbled rocks that made up the arms of the miniature bay.

Carol followed Loren from the cockpit down into the cabin. The yacht rocked gently, and Carol could hear the water slapping lightly against the hull. Loren turned to face her. "What do you want?"

The jolt of desire caught Carol by surprise. "You," she heard herself say.

She could taste the salt spray on Loren's lips. Balanced on the fulcrum between advance or withdrawal, Carol hesitated, then acquiesced. She'd forgotten what it was like to kiss someone new, someone whose mouth she had never tasted, never explored with her tongue. She found herself more eager for this discovery than she could believe, more willing to abandon all restraint.

"Wow!" said Loren, drawing back.

"Let's not stop."

Her face lit with a smile, Loren asked, "All the way? Are you game?"

A tremor passed through Carol's body, as though she were casting off a tightness, a chilly reserve. "I'm game for anything," she said, hardly recognizing her own husky voice.

Laughing in her arms, Loren said, "The bunk will be a tight fit."

"The tighter the better."

Carol was peripherally conscious of the gentle movement of the yacht as it tugged at the anchor and of the distant cry of gulls. But overlaying all else was a sweeping flow of sensory overload that scorched her with its intensity. Had ever bare skin felt so impossibly erotic? Had ever desire transfixed her, filled her, pierced her like this?

"Hurry," Carol said. "I don't believe I can wait."

They stood kissing, removing the last of their clothes. Now there were no barriers between them, no boundaries to the exquisite carnal dance they had begun.

"I've dreamed of doing this," whispered Loren. "And more, much more." Her mouth was hot, demanding, her hands sure.

Carol was dissolving, flowing, burning. "Shall we lie down, my captain, or will you take me here?" she gasped, the laughter bubbling in her throat.

"As you stand," murmured Loren against her throat. Carol welcomed Loren within her, the rhythm driving her to the brink. She tried to hold back, to keep the ecstasy of the moment, but there was no stopping the relentless clamor for release. Carol shouted with the joy of it, with the exultation that filled her as she surrendered everything — her body, herself.

Then they made love in the cramped bunk. Jammed up against the bulkhead, Carol felt safe and daring all at once. Loren's skin was silky, her responses unbridled, her voice choked with desire as she urged Carol on, instructed her, pleaded with her. Higher, farther, wilder. For those moments Carol almost accepted that they would die from passion. That their beating hearts would burst.

* * * * *

Half-dressed, they sat in the cockpit and devoured the contents of the luncheon basket Loren had brought. Carol stretched luxuriously. She felt playful, mischievous. "I don't generally do more than a chaste kiss on the first date," she said. "You've led me astray."

Loren saluted her with her plastic tumbler of wine. "I'd be delighted to take you even farther from the path of virtue."

A sudden gust caught the yacht broadside, swinging it on the anchor. The temperature was dropping, and dark clouds were racing across the sky. Carol could smell rain in the air. "We'd better get back, a storm is coming."

The direction of the wind had reversed, so they raced before it all the way to the marina. Carol looked back to see the flash of lightning forking through the roiling clouds, followed by the distant rumble of thunder. "Just in time," she called to Loren.

They docked under engine power, secured the sails, gathered their things and locked the cabin just as huge drops began to splash on the deck. Laughing, they bolted for shelter as the rain began in earnest. Huddled under the nearest awning, they waited for a break in the downfall. Carol looked at the woman beside her. *With just one touch*, she thought, *you can ignite me. But I really don't know anything about you.*

"Come back to my place," she said. "I'm in the middle of alterations, but the bathroom works, so you can have a hot shower."

She was unaccountably relieved when Loren shook her head, saying that she had to meet the magazine photographer at her hotel. "Lunch tomorrow, Carol?

I've found a great Italian restaurant near the beach at Bondi."

Carol intended to go into work on Sunday, but she was determined to arrange things so she could have time with Loren. "How about an early dinner?" They arranged to meet the next day, and when the rain slacked off, they went to their respective cars.

As Carol drove home she realized why she'd had a feeling of relief when Loren had refused her invitation. In some sense Sybil's presence was still in her house, the ghost of a relationship that had meant so much. Carol turned into her carport and turned off the ignition. She sat looking at the water trickling down the glass, thinking about Sybil. She got out and slammed the car door harder than she intended. She was over Sybil. And Sybil was definitely over her.

Sweeping Sinker into her arms when he greeted her at the front door, she said, "You love me, don't you?" He gave a gurgle that she interrupted as an affirmative answer. She put him down and they walked together down the hall.

Carol's skin still tingled from Loren's touch. She was impatient to see her again. Was this the beginning of something? Or was this just a pleasant dalliance, an antidote to loneliness?

CHAPTER SEVENTEEN

A phone call from the commissioner advised Carol that she was to meet with Dick Juno on Sunday afternoon to fill him in with the details of the possible danger to his life. Juno had flown in on his private jet and was staying on his lavish vessel, aptly named *Entrepreneur*, that had been scheduled to dock in Sydney Harbour in time for his arrival.

The squall of Saturday afternoon had blown itself into a full-scale storm. A high wind keened in the trees, and the streets ran with torrents of water. Carol's wipers could barely cope with the gray sheets of rain buffeting her car. With difficulty she found Juno's vessel berthed at a city pier. Squeezing into a parking spot, she made a dash for the shelter of the old two-level wharf.

Dick Juno's security arrangements were adequate. First she was checked at the entrance gate, then directed to further guards at the foot of the gangplank. A hard-faced young woman who looked as if she'd majored in martial arts went through the contents of Carol's briefcase, then asked her to step through a metal detector before escorting her up the covered gangplank.

Even lashed by rain, the luxury of *Entrepreneur* was obvious. The wet brass gleamed, the decks were snowy white, and, once inside, Carol caught a glimpse of crew members in immaculate uniforms. There was the faint smell of polish in the tepid air. Carol was ushered through a richly gleaming wooden door into a reception room thickly carpeted in white.

"Inspector Ashton," announced the young woman, then she left, closing the door quietly behind her.

Dick Juno leapt up to greet Carol. "I'm so pleased you could come," he said, as though she were an invited guest. Shaking her hand firmly, he went on, "Your commissioner tells me I'm in danger."

Juno inclined his head toward a bulky man standing by the black-and-chrome bar. He was wearing a tight brown suit and had a neck so thick it seemed part of his shoulders. "Nick will look after me, won't you Nick?"

His bodyguard grunted an assent.

Dick Juno was slightly built, with a head of thick brown hair and a trim body. Carol had seen him on television, and recognized his signature boyish manner, which suggested that everything he did was an escapade that delighted him. She had been prepared to dislike him intensely, but it was difficult to match this ebullient man with the rampart capitalist who had caused so much willful destruction.

"Please make yourself comfortable." He sat opposite Carol on a white leather chair, leaning forward with an expression of keen interest. "What can you tell me?"

Carol handed Juno photographs of Fitch, Bonnie d'Arlene and Phoebe. "Do you recognize any of these people?"

"No to this one. And this one." He tapped Bonnie's face. "This one I know. A fanatic. Turned up in the middle of the Amazon with a film crew. I soon sent her packing." He laid a finger along the side of his nose. "Had the local authorities in my pocket, you see."

The dislike Carol hadn't felt before suddenly blossomed. "Did you have any direct contact with Ms. d'Arlene?" she asked.

"Did I speak with her, do you mean?" Juno snorted a laugh. "Christ, I've got enough to do without wasting my valuable time on someone like her."

"So that's a no?"

His grin was disarming. "It's a no, Inspector."

"Bonnie d'Arlene is in Sydney at the moment."

Juno considered Carol's statement. "Could you arrest her?" he asked with a note of polite inquiry.

"She hasn't done anything to warrant that."

Dick Juno gave Carol a knowing look. "I'm sure there's some charge that could be brought. Perhaps a problem with customs? A passport irregularity?"

"Creative arrest?" said Carol, raising her eyebrows. "I'm afraid not."

He shrugged. "If you say so." He gestured toward the bar. "Would you like something to drink?"

"Thank you, no."

"You'll forgive me if I have a Scotch." Juno gestured to Nick, who lumbered behind the bar with the waddle of a bodybuilder whose thighs were over-developed. It seemed it was a task Nick had down to a fine art, as Juno had a crystal glass in his hand within a few moments.

He swished the amber liquid in a circular move-ment, the ice cubes clicking with a cool sound. A quick mouthful, then he said, "A serial killer targeting businessmen like me? Do you really think that's feasible?"

"I'd hate to have you prove the point," said Carol. "All we ask is that you take extra precautions. Don't stick to a set routine, and don't publicize your move-ments."

Cradling his drink, he considered her with a faint smile. "You don't look like a cop," he said.

Ignoring his remark, Carol indicated the floor-to-ceiling windows that made up the front wall of the area. "I suggest you avoid that part of the room, especially at night."

"Why?"

She pointed through the rain-speckled glass to the upper level of the pier. "A sharpshooter up there would only need one clear view of you." She added conversationally, "It'd be a head shot, to take you down for good."

Clearly taken aback, Juno said, "I've got trained

security to look after anything like that." He tipped back his head to finish his Scotch with a long swallow, then handed the glass to Nick. "Another one."

"Do you mind if I smoke?" Without waiting for Carol's response he gave a quick nod to Nick, who came over with a humidor. Selecting a fat cigar, Juno busied himself with the business of smelling it, snipping off the end with a tiny gold guillotine, then turning it as he lit it with an onyx lighter.

When he had assured himself that the cigar was burning satisfactorily, he took the second Scotch from Nick and leaned back comfortably in his chair. "Tell me about these murders."

Carol had been instructed to explain to Juno why his life might be in danger, so she gave him a summary of the cases, concentrating on Banning and Rad Danvers, but also mentioning the possibility that both Cardover and Guthrie were victims of the same murderer.

He listened carefully, nodding occasionally. When she had finished he said, "Cardover I'd heard of, but never met. Walter Banning I knew well. We had common interests, and he beat me out of one very profitable deal." His mouth tightened. "Very profitable." From his tone Carol gathered that Banning's death was unlikely to cause Juno a moment's concern. "And I've never heard of the others," he added with a shrug.

"Do you know the members of your crew?"

Blinking at her question, he said, "Most of them, I suppose."

"It would be wise to check if any new people have been hired in the last few months."

For the first time Juno seemed to be taking the

situation seriously. "You think someone would go to those lengths? Besides, you said yourself the murderer has been finding his victims here in Sydney, and this vessel's been at sea for several weeks. Whoever it is can't be in two places at once."

"That only works if there is just one person doing the killing."

He stared at Carol. "You're telling me there's more than one loony involved?"

"It's possible."

With a sound of disgust, he said, "Jesus Christ! Take off the kid gloves and arrest the bastards." He heaved himself out of his chair and began to pace around the room, gesturing with his half-full glass of Scotch. "Pathetic losers, the whole bunch of them. Whining about the bloody environment as if they personally owned it." He swung around to Carol. "What do you think of them, yourself? Off the record."

"I think you might underestimate them, and that could be fatal. Literally."

He smiled at her cool reply. "Would you like to stay for dinner and discuss this over a meal? I assure you my chef is excellent."

"I have another appointment."

"Do you, indeed?" Juno's smile widened. "You know, I could request you as my personal bodyguard. Do you think your top cop would agree to that?"

Carol had spent a couple of hours with Mark Bourke going over the status of each case. There'd been a report of a sighting of Phoebe Yarmelle near Nowra, but that had turned out to be a false lead.

Feeling a bit guilty, she left him working and drove to meet Loren at Bondi.

The restaurant was a little Italian café with red-and-white checkered tablecloths and an enthusiastic clientele. The smells of delicious food filled the room. A waiter with a truly magnificent mustache seated them at a cramped table wedged in a corner. Carol took a cautious sip of the house red that Loren insisted would impart a genuine Italian flavor to their meal.

"So how was Dick Juno?" Loren asked.

"Insufferable. He's so used to getting his own way he thought all he needed to do was say he wanted me appointed as his personal bodyguard and it'd be a fait accompli."

"You weren't keen?"

"I was not."

Loren gave her a wicked smile. "I'd have you as my bodyguard any day. Any night, in fact."

Carol felt a pleasant tingle of anticipation. She was about to reply when their food was set in front of them with a flourish. The beaming waiter crooned a few words in Italian, to which Loren replied. An animated conversation ensued before he was called away.

"I didn't realize you spoke Italian," said Carol, thinking how little she did know about Loren's background.

"I'm good at languages. A natural mimic, that's me."

Carol surveyed her heaped plate ruefully. "Why can I never resist ordering spaghetti? It's impossible to eat it with any semblance of style."

Loren sprinkled a generous portion of Parmesan

cheese over her pasta. "I'd say you do everything with style, Carol. Even spaghetti." She took a mouthful, and an expression of bliss appeared on her face. "This is good."

After a few moments, Loren said, "Tell me all about Dick Juno."

"Why? He's arrogant and rich. What's more to say?"

"I'd love to swing an interview with him. He's good copy, Carol, however odious he is at the personal level."

Carol's mobile phone chirped in her purse. It always seemed to her to be the height of pretension to chat away on a phone in the middle of a restaurant, but there was no way she could extricate herself quickly from the corner in which they were wedged, so she apologized to Loren and took the call.

"Bonnie and Fitch have disappeared," said Bourke. "They obviously knew they were being watched, and they slipped the tail."

Carol hadn't had the personnel to set up a tight surveillance, and her intention had been more directed toward picking up Phoebe Yarmelle if she tried to contact the Gaia's Revenge leaders. "What about the tap on the phones?"

"Not a thing, Carol. Fitch and Bonnie d'Arlene might look like amateurs, but they're not. If they don't want to be found, they won't be."

"This is just great," said Carol. "We've got three possible suspects running around loose, and one inviting target."

"Would they go for the obvious?" said Bourke. "I mean, while we're obsessing about Dick Juno, it'd be a perfect chance to pick off some other worthy victim.

From their point of view there's no shortage of potential kills."

"Advise Juno to step up his security anyway, Mark. He's sailing out of Sydney on Wednesday morning, weather permitting, so he'll only be our responsibility for a couple more days."

"Sorry," she said to Loren, putting the phone away.

"Problems?"

"Nothing I can discuss."

A slow smile spread over Loren's face. "You're quite a challenge," she said. "You'd be astonished how much people will reveal when I'm interviewing them for an article. Sometimes they remember to say whatever they're telling me is off the record, but mostly people just open up and talk. You're not like that."

"Would you want me to be?"

"Carol, I wouldn't change you in any way."

When they left the restaurant, the rain was still pouring. Carol always refused to carry an umbrella, but she was willing to huddle under Loren's as they hurried to Carol's car.

"I'm glad I took a taxi here," said Loren, shaking water from her hair. "And didn't use my rental car. It's bad enough driving on the wrong side of the road, but add weather like this and I'd run someone down in a second."

From her observations, Carol doubted this was true. Loren seemed to do everything with brisk efficiency. "Where do you want to go?" she asked.

Loren looked surprised at the question. "We're going back to my hotel, aren't we?" She put a hand on Carol's knee. "I was hoping to show you a little more of my repertoire."

"Hell," said Carol as she turned on the wipers, "if it keeps raining like this, my builder will finish my alterations some time next year, and that's if I'm lucky."

She flipped on the radio to catch the weather forecast, picking up the middle of a an item on Dick Juno. "A keen sailor," said the announcer, "Dick Juno is considering the entry of his radical new yacht in the Sydney to Hobart yacht race on New Year's Day."

The forecast followed, and it was not encouraging. A gale warning was out for the southern New South Wales coast, and the low was expected to intensify over the next forty-eight hours.

"I love weather like this," said Loren. "Have you ever been sailing in a real storm?"

"I've been caught out on the water a couple of times, and I didn't enjoy the experience." Basically, Carol thought, she didn't like rain. She could put up with a couple of wet days, but any period longer than that made her gloomy and impatient.

Loren's hotel was dry, welcoming, and full of understated elegance. In daylight her room would have a lovely view over the Royal Botanic Gardens and Farm Cove. Tonight the wet darkness crowded against the glass.

Loren ordered French champagne, "To make up for that rather rough red wine," she explained. When it arrived with two chilled glasses, she insisted on opening it herself.

Watching her deftly ease the cork out of the bottle, Carol wanted to relax and enjoy herself, but nagging doubts about the investigation plucked at her mind. Had she missed something in the series of murders? Perhaps Banning and Danvers were linked in some way she hadn't noticed. Had she taken the right steps? Covered all the bases? Perhaps she'd been too eager to believe that the Gaia's Revenge organization was involved.

"What's worrying you?" asked Loren, pouring the champagne.

"Just the cases I'm working on. Can't turn off my head."

Loren handed her a glass. "I've got a remedy for that," she said. "I guarantee you'll not be able to think straight for quite some time."

Sleeping, Loren looked much younger. Carol, lying naked beside her, traced a line with one finger down the curve of her back. Loren stirred, smiled, opened her eyes, the alert intelligence snapping back into her face. "Are you staying all night?"

"I have to go home to get a change of clothes. And to catch the builder. The least he can do is finish the inside work if it's still raining." Carol didn't mention Sinker. She'd left him plenty of food, and she was sure he'd entertained himself by getting into all the places normally forbidden to him.

"Before you go," said Loren, putting her arms around Carol's neck, "one last time."

They were still learning the mysteries of each other's bodies, but it was a steep learning curve. Carol had never had a lover so vocal, so unself-consciously abandoned. Nor one so sexually demanding.

"What are you smiling at?" Loren asked.

"I was just thinking you're too much for me," said Carol.

She expected a flippant reply, but Loren raised herself on one elbow and looked seriously into Carol's face. "I'm not enough for you," she said. She leaned forward and kissed Carol gently. "Not nearly enough."

CHAPTER EIGHTEEN

"I spoke to Dick Juno himself last night," said
Bourke. "He treated the whole thing as a bit of a
joke. Made some reference to basket-weaving eco-
freaks."

Carol smothered a yawn, and picked up her mug.
The jolt of caffeine would have to stand in for the
sleep she'd missed. "Tom Keys has an article on
Gerald Fitch and Gaia's Revenge in this morning's
paper," she said. "I only glanced at it, but it seemed a
bit of a send-up. It seems nobody's taking him very
seriously."

"The current theory the media subscribe to is that we have a celebrity serial killer loose," said Bourke with a cynical smile. "And since ordinary people feel safe, they're enjoying the idea that someone is picking off the sinfully rich or, in the case of Danvers, a mad scientist who does nasty things to innocent animals."

Carol rubbed her forehead to forestall the headache she felt starting. "We aren't any further ahead than we were when Walter Banning was killed," she said. "I can't help feeling we're being set up, maybe by Bonnie d'Arlene and company."

"They're just seizing the opportunity for free publicity," said Bourke. "I really can't see them organizing these murders. Whoever's responsible is pretty smart."

"Or lucky," said Carol.

Loren, looking as if she'd had a refreshing night's sleep, came into Carol's office. "Got a moment?"

Bourke stayed for a few minutes to chat, then took himself off. Loren sat in the chair he'd vacated. "I'm afraid I can't see you this evening. I've got a revised deadline on an eco-tourism article, and I'll have to finish it tonight."

"I'm disappointed," said Carol, "but maybe a good night's sleep is what I need."

Loren looked at her reflectively. "What do you think of Gaia's Revenge?"

"The organization, or the idea behind it?"

"Both."

Carol picked up her gold pen and fiddled with it. Loren's expression made it clear she expected a serious reply, so Carol reflected before she said, "I have to admit I rather admire people who believe things strongly enough to put themselves on the line. And I support environmental concerns in general. I'm not sure that radical actions are the way to go, and obviously I can't agree with breaking the law, even though I can sympathize with some of the motives people have when they do it."

"What about the execution of Rad Danvers?"

Carol gave her a half-smile. "*Execution?* Using that word justifies the action. Dr. Danvers was murdered."

"And the animals he experimented upon? Weren't they tortured and eventually murdered to provide information for whatever drug company paid Danvers to do it?"

Carol grimaced. The cages with the dead chimps had affected her more than she had realized at the time. "Experiments like that are horrible, and if they're unnecessary, they should be banned. As for Danvers, I can't help feeling the world is a better place without him, but that doesn't condone his murder."

Loren nodded, as though Carol had said what she expected her to say. "Let's meet this evening, before I go off to work for my living."

Carol was at her desk all day, and by late afternoon she was tired and discouraged. The last week and a half had been the most frustrating of her career. The murders had followed each other so quickly, and, she had to admit, so efficiently: Walter Banning shot; Eric Cardover given a fatal injection; Rad Danvers shot. As for the death of Edward Guthrie, she was convinced that there would never be definite proof one way or the other, so his case would stay in the files as an accidental shooting.

If something happened to Dick Juno, that would be the fourth murder in the space of a few days. In the whole of New South Wales the total murders for a year averaged less than a hundred, and Carol wasn't looking for her cases to create a statistical anomaly.

At six she packed up and went to meet Loren in the local coffee shop that was one of Carol's favorites. It wasn't busy, probably because of the rain that was sullenly falling, so they had an area all to themselves. Loren was pensive, and Carol made most of the conversation. At seven Loren checked her watch. "I'm sorry, but I really do have to go."

Outside, before they parted, she gave Carol a hug and a quick kiss. Carol watched her walk off with her confident, loose-limbed stride. She turned to wave, then she was gone.

The next morning at the children's court was a trying experience. The noisy hallways were full of the smell of damp clothes, Carol had been stabbed by at least two umbrellas, and most of the people thronging the public area seemed to be worried or defiant, or both. She'd been waiting half an hour when Justin strode in with David and Eleanor. "Our man here yet?" he asked Carol, raising his voice over the noise.

"I've no idea." She gestured to the crowded hallway. "Half the world seems to be scheduled for this morning."

Carol had been to the children's court before, but always in her position as a police officer. It was quite different as a parent, finding oneself at the beck and call of officials. She put an arm around David, who was quiet and rather pale. "It'll be over soon."

Julian stalked off, to reappear in a few minutes later. "It's all set. We're on at ten." He clapped his son on the shoulder. "Never put us through this again."

Once they were in the courtroom the whole process was over very quickly. David admitted his guilt, papers were perused, a stern lecture given, and, as this was his first brush with the law, he was released into the care of his custodial parent.

David perked up once they were outside. "That wasn't so bad," he said, as if his voice hadn't trembled when he'd spoken in court. Seeing Carol's expression, he added hastily, "I did take it seriously, Mum."

Carol declined Justin and Eleanor's offer of lunch, reminded David that he'd promised to ring Aunt Sarah and Sybil to tell them both how his appearance had gone, and, after giving him a quick hug, she splashed her way to her car. The rain had eased, but the last forecast she'd heard that morning had promised wilder weather ahead.

Frowning, she punched in the number of Loren's hotel. Last night, on impulse, she tried to call her, but had got the hotel voice-mail service. Carol had figured that Loren wasn't accepting calls, but again this morning there'd been no answer. She left another voice-mail message.

Then she called Bourke. "I'll be there in half an hour. Anything urgent?"

"You've got a message to ring someone called Nick Parmentis."

A tingle of alarm prickled her skin. "That's Dick Juno's personal bodyguard. Did he say what he wanted?"

"No. Just that he wanted to speak with you."

She took the number and called it immediately. The bodyguard answered on the second ring. "Nick here."

"This is Inspector Carol Ashton. You wanted me?"

"Yeah. Mr. Juno's been out all night. And I haven't heard from him this morning. That's very unusual."

"Where did he go?"

Nick rumbled a laugh. "Had a date with a pretty lady. Didn't ask me along. I'd have been in the way."

"Do you know her name?"

This question amused him further. "Jesus, no. Mr. Juno's arrangements are always private. I didn't even see her."

"A call girl?"

"I suppose. She'll be good-looking. Mr. Juno likes blonds. Perhaps you noticed he took a shine to you."

"Isn't it possible he took a hotel room for the night, and he's still there?"

"No way. Mr. Juno had important business calls this morning. He wouldn't have missed them. Something's wrong."

"Detective Sergeant Bourke will call you back shortly. Give him every bit of information you have. I'll meet you at the pier in twenty minutes. I want to interview anyone who saw Mr. Juno leave yesterday."

Carol called Bourke and told him to contact Nick after he'd advised Superintendent Edgar that Juno was missing. "Somehow I doubt it's a kidnaping, but I want Juno's phones monitored. Get a team down there fast."

She started her car and pulled into the stream of traffic stop-starting its way through the flooded streets. She wasn't surprised at Juno having a date with a call girl, even though she conceivably could be a plant, but what did confound her was that he freely left the security of his boat, even though he'd been expressly warned to be careful. He had a reputation as a thrill seeker, and Carol wryly thought that maybe this time he'd looked for one thrill too many.

Of course there was every possibility that Nick was wrong, and that Juno was off somewhere with a pliant bedmate, but all Carol instincts told her that something unpleasant had happened to him. Who could lure Juno away to kill him? Bonnie d'Arlene wasn't a possibility. Not only did he know her, she was hardly the type he went for. Phoebe Yarmelle was another matter. Carol could imagine Juno being attracted to her wide blue eyes and little-girl voice.

Nick, his face set in a scowl of concern, met her at the bottom of the gangplank. "Something's happened to him, I know it," he said. "Should have taken me with him, girl or no girl."

"Sergeant Bourke will be checking hospitals to make sure Mr. Juno wasn't in an accident." She didn't mention Bourke would also be checking the morgue.

Nick took her up to the same reception room where she'd met Juno on Sunday. "The people you wanted," he said.

The hard-faced young woman was there, together with an older man in overalls and a snappily uniformed officer.

"Mr. Juno went out alone after seven. It was raining and dark, but he didn't even ask for his car," said the woman before Carol could frame a question.

"Did he say anything to indicate where he was going?"

She hesitated, then said, "I heard him on the phone. He was making arrangements to meet someone."

"A man or a woman?" asked Carol.

A faint smile crossed her face. "A woman. He was chatting her up. I think she was daring him to do something. I don't know what."

The other two confirmed that Mr. Juno had come down the gangplank dressed in jeans and a leather jacket and had walked off whistling. That was the last any of them had seen of him.

"Did he call in for messages during the evening?"

That drew a negative response. Carol asked a few more questions, but it was obvious that there was nothing more to be learned. "I'm arranging for all calls to and from the boat to be monitored," she said to Nick.

He shook his heavy head. "If you're thinking kidnaping, you're wrong. No one's asking for money, and they would have, by now." His face lugubrious, he said, "He's dead. I know it."

Back in her car, Carol mentally shuddered at the media onslaught Dick Juno's disappearance would cause. She was half listening to a news digest on her radio when the announcer declared she had an important breaking story. "Unconfirmed reports indicate that multimillionaire businessman Dick Juno may have been kidnaped. Mr. Juno is at present visiting Sydney for business reasons, and to finalize the entry of his new maxi-yacht, *Capitalist's Dream,* currently undergoing sea trials at San Diego, California, in the grueling Sydney to Hobart ocean race."

San Diego, California. Carol had been there as a tourist. The city was just above the border with Mexico. Loren had said she had grown up there in sight of the sea.

"Oh, God," said Carol.

CHAPTER NINETEEN

Carol went straight to her desk and took out the bio on Loren she'd crammed into her top drawer. Her stomach turned over as she checked the pages. *Born in Yorba Linda, California. Attended UCLA.* What had Loren said when she was assuring Carol that she was an expert sailor? She could hear her voice saying, "I grew up in San Diego, California, and I could sail almost before I could walk."

Carol found Sam Goolwa eating a bacon-and-egg sandwich at his desk, and instructed him to contact the States and check out the biographical information down to the last detail. "It's the middle of the night there," he protested.

"I don't care who you wake up. This is the highest priority."

Then she spent a frustrating twenty minutes locating someone in charge at the marina where Loren's borrowed yacht was moored. When she finished that call she felt physically sick. Loren hadn't borrowed the yacht *Sea Song* from a friend; rather, she had paid a considerable sum to lease it for a month. And it was missing from its berth. "Jesus," the guy at the marina had said, "I wouldn't go out in this weather if you paid me a million bucks."

The manager at Loren's hotel was reluctant, but after a terse conversation with him, Carol dispatched Anne Newsome to the hotel. "The manager's expecting you. He'll let you into Loren Reece's room. Have a look around and then call me. Use your mobile phone, and don't touch anything."

Bourke came in while she was briefing Anne. "Carol, what is it?" he said, concerned.

"Loren Reece. I hope I'm wrong, but I can't locate her, there are inconsistencies in her background story, and a yacht she chartered is not at its mooring."

"You're kidding me, aren't you?" He ran a hand over his face. "She got Dick Juno's unlisted number from me."

Superintendent Edgar appeared at the door. "What the bloody hell's going on, Carol? How did the media get hold of this Juno story so fast? And what are you doing to locate the man?"

He listened to Carol's outline of the situation with growing impatience. "That's rubbish about Loren

Reece. She not only knows the premier, she's an accredited international journalist, for God's sake!"

After a few more blistering comments, he stalked off, snapping over his shoulder, "And keep me informed. Every detail."

Bourke made a face at his retreating back. "No wonder he's upset. The commissioner's going to come down on him like a load of bricks." He turned back to Carol. "I'll send Miles Li to the marina. Maybe someone saw something useful."

"Have we got a photo of Loren he could take?"

"There wasn't one with her bio. I'll check with the premier's PR department."

Carol had a sudden snapshot image of the television cameras outside Rad Danvers's building, and of Loren shielding her face with an open umbrella. "I don't think there'll be any photos," she said.

Anne called in with the expected news: Loren Reece had packed most of her clothes and taken her passport and other papers with her. Her room held no personal items, no scraps of paper, nothing of interest. The manager was complaining, but Anne had secured the room, and technicians were dusting the furniture for fingerprints.

A full alert was out for the *Sea Song*. The coast guard had been advised, although the gale force winds and huge seas made the location of one small vessel very difficult. A search of the myriad coves and inlets of Sydney Harbour had been instituted, in case the yacht had been quietly taken to an empty mooring.

The afternoon newscasts all featured Gerald Fitch and Bonnie d'Arlene, who had resurfaced to make provocative statements about Dick Juno. With patent insincerity, they both said how they hoped Mr. Juno had not come to personal harm, but they implied clearly that his activities had been so destructive that in some mythic way the earth had had her revenge. In the same newscasts, Juno's company offered a ten-million-dollar reward for his safe return.

Carol hadn't eaten lunch. She felt as if she would never want to eat anything again. She was staring morosely at a chicken sandwich that Bourke had put on her desk together with a paper cup of genuine coffee he'd bought from a coffee shop when he came in to tell her that Phoebe Yarmelle was waiting outside.

This was a different Phoebe to the woman Carol had first met. She had on sneakers, jeans and a sweater, wore no makeup, and had her thick chestnut hair pulled back in a ponytail.

"Perhaps you've been looking for me," she said, her glance going from Bourke to Carol. Her voice was the same: high and light, and somehow innocent. Innocence, however, was the last thing Carol would attribute to Phoebe Yarmelle.

"You know Loren Reece, as she calls herself," Carol said bluntly.

"No, I don't." Her expression dared Carol to contradict her. Phoebe went on matter-of-factly, "I imagine you will be interested to know if I have an alibi that will cover the time of Mr. Juno's disappearance. I do have such an alibi, and I'll be delighted to give it to you."

A faint smile touched her lips. "I've been in Queensland for the past forty-eight hours. Yesterday I managed to get myself arrested during a demon-

stration outside the Brisbane offices of Edward
Guthrie's company. Perhaps you remember his recent
accidental death. Anyway, I was in the custody of the
police until my appearance in court this morning,
when I posted bail. I arrived in Sydney an hour ago
by a Qantas flight. Here's my ticket."

Carol let Bourke question her further, but it was
obvious that her alibi was rock solid. Bourke saw her
out, then came back to say, "We've been played like
fish on a line. It was all a setup."

Carol, tired to the bone, nodded. "That amateur
group, Gaia's Revenge, has accomplished a very professional conspiracy. I don't doubt that they're all
involved, Fitch, Bonnie d'Arlene and Phoebe Yarmelle,
but as long as they stick together, we'll have a hard
time proving it."

"Money may be the key," said Bourke. "They must
have paid Loren plenty."

Loren. The very sound of her name stung Carol's
ears. She felt hollow, insubstantial, as though all this
was happening to someone else. There was no hard
evidence — there might never be hard evidence — but
Carol knew with a cold certainty that twice Loren had
left her and gone to kill a victim.

After their first dinner together, Loren had said
good-bye to Carol at the entrance to the hotel, then
slipped out and gone to Ultimo to kill Rad Danvers.
And last night, when she had turned and waved to
Carol, she had been on her way to meet, and murder,
Dick Juno.

With an effort she wrenched her mind back to the
business at hand. "You've started advising the overseas
authorities? Interpol? No doubt there'll be cor-

respondences between some of the victims on the death list on Gaia's Web site and Loren Reece's arrival in various countries."

"I still don't believe it," said Bourke. He gave a rueful laugh. "God, she was so bloody *nice*."

By late afternoon Goolwa had answers from the United States. Bourke and Carol studied the pages together in silence. When she was six, Loren Reece, the only child of William and Robyn Reece, had died with her parents in a railway crossing accident. Five years ago, using the dead Loren Reece's birth certificate and her social security number, someone had built up a false identity, applying for a California driver license and a passport, and establishing a bank account and credit cards.

The woman who called herself Loren Reece had also created dummy employment records, but she was an undeniably talented journalist who actually had worked for some of the publications she quoted in her résumé. Whatever her real name, she was, in fact, an established freelance writer, respected in her field.

Just before dark, wreckage of a yacht was sighted off the coast north of Sydney. Dick Juno's body wasn't discovered until the next morning, wedged in shoreline rocks by the pounding waves. He'd been shot in the head.

Splintered by the force of the ocean, the remains of the *Sea Song* washed ashore over the next few days. Loren Reece's body wasn't found.

CHAPTER TWENTY

Carol ruffled her son's hair. "All finished," she said, surveying her house with a sigh of satisfaction. The spring air of the Saturday morning was warm, the birds were singing, and the last of Kev's sheds had been dismantled and taken away.

Aunt Sarah, white hair fluffed around her tanned face, waved barbecue tongs in Carol's direction. "Time to light the fire? When's everyone arriving?"

"I said twelve," said Carol. "That means Mark and Pat will be here ten minutes early, but it still gives us a good hour."

Carol scorned gas barbecues and had built her own with bricks and a large sheet of heavy steel. The only drawback was that the fire had to be made and nurtured long before the food was cooked. She and David had collected armfuls of kindling from the bush that morning and stacked it ready for use.

"I'll make up the fire," said David.

Aunt Sarah relinquished the barbecue and joined Carol. "Did you ask Sybil?"

"Yes." She frowned at the enthusiasm on her aunt's face. "She's coming as a friend, that's all." Carol didn't add how surprised she had been when Sybil had accepted the invitation to celebrate the completion of the house with a gathering of friends.

"It's a start," said Aunt Sarah. She put up a hand. "Okay, I won't say another word on the subject."

They strolled together, inspecting the newly landscaped gardens. "You're too thin," said Aunt Sarah. "That Reece case really took it out of you, didn't it?"

"It was tough." That was an understatement, Carol thought. Months of painstaking work had had very little result. There had been no identifiable fingerprints in Loren's hotel room. Carol had hoped to trace the paintings Loren had bought from Pat's gallery to friends who might know something about her, but had found that Loren had donated the artworks to a local animal shelter that had been holding an auction for funds.

Carol hadn't been able to find any concrete link between Loren and Gaia's Revenge, although she was convinced that they had been working closely together. And the persona of Loren Reece had melted away to nothing when examined closely, both in Australia and overseas. Loren had moved easily in a web of contacts and friends who thought they knew her well, but when it came down to it, no one had.

The Banning, Cardover and Juno cases remained open, but Carol had no expectation they would ever be officially solved. Carol believed that Jonathan Cardover had been ambitious and uncaring, but she no longer had any thought that he'd been involved in his father's death.

Suspicions about Loren's involvement in overseas cases remained, but these, too, seemed never likely to be resolved, even though in several instances records showed that Loren had been in the particular country at the critical time.

The media had been eager to paint Loren Reece as "a beautiful, yet deadly woman," who had assumed the role of avenger for the destruction of the natural world. The furor had died down, but Carol was sure the story would be resurrected at regular intervals, becoming more lurid each time.

Carol glanced at her watch. "I'm expecting an e-mail from the States. It's still Friday there." Carol had been encouraged to apply for an intensive FBI training course designed to profile serial killers. The commissioner himself had given her application his blessing, and she knew that this was in part because of the embarrassment the Reece case had caused the force.

Part of her was reluctant, but a tickle of excitement was there too. It would be a demanding course, but it would also be an escape from the pressures and expectations that dogged her every day. Carol was clear-sighted enough to realize that she was so accustomed to success that her recent failure was all the more bitter and demoralizing.

She settled herself at the kitchen bench and logged on her portable computer. With a jolt of anticipation she saw the Federal Bureau of Investigation in the list of messages waiting. Before opening it, she scanned the rest quickly. Junk mail, an international police newsletter she subscribed to, and electronic letters from a couple of friends. There was one she didn't recognize. She idly clicked on, then sat transfixed.

I never wanted to say good-bye to you. I think of you every day. Miss you every day. If there is ever any way in the future we can meet, I'll make it happen, Carol. In all my world, in all my experiences, you are the one.

Carol didn't need to read the name at the bottom. *Loren.*

INTIMATE STRANGER by Laura DeHart Young. 192 pp.
Ignoring Tray's myserious past, could Cole be playing with fire?
ISBN 1-56280-249-6 $11.95

SHATTERED ILLUSIONS by Kaye Davis. 256 pp. 4th
Maris Middleton mystery.   ISBN 1-56280-252-6   11.95

SETUP by Claire McNab. 224 pp. 11th Detective Inspector Carol
Ashton mystery.   ISBN 1-56280-255-0   11.95

THE DAWNING by Laura Adams. 224 pp. What if you had the
power to change the past?   ISBN 1-56280-246-1   11.95

NEVER ENDING by Marianne Martin. 224 pp. Temptation
appears in the form of an old friend and lover. ISBN 1-56280-247-X   11.95

ONE OF OUR OWN by Diane Salvatore. 240 pp. Carly Matson
has a secret. So does Lela Johns.   ISBN 1-56280-243-7   11.95

DOUBLE TAKEOUT by Tracey Richardson. 176 pp. 3rd Stevie
Houston mystery.   ISBN 1-56280-244-5   11.95

CAPTIVE HEART by Frankie J. Jones. 176 pp. Love in the
fast lane or heartside romance?   ISBN 1-56280-258-5   11.95

WICKED GOOD TIME by Diana Tremain Braund. 224 pp. In
charge at work, out of control in her heart.   ISBN 1-56280-241-0   11.95

SNAKE EYES by Pat Welch. 256 pp. 7th Helen Black mystery.
ISBN 1-56280-242-9   11.95

CHANGE OF HEART by Linda Hill. 176 pp. High fashion and
love in a glamorous world.   ISBN 1-56280-238-0   11.95

UNSTRUNG HEART by Robbi Sommers. 176 pp. Putting life
in order again.   ISBN 1-56280-239-9   11.95

BIRDS OF A FEATHER by Jackie Calhoun. 240 pp. Life begins
with love.   ISBN 1-56280-240-2   11.95

THE DRIVE by Trisha Todd. 176 pp. The star of *Claire of the
Moon* tells all!   ISBN 1-56280-237-2   11.95

BOTH SIDES by Saxon Bennett. 240 pp. A community of
women falling in and out of love.   ISBN 1-56280-236-4   11.95

WATERMARK by Karin Kallmaker. 256 pp. One burning
question . . . how to lead her back to love?   ISBN 1-56280-235-6   11.95

THE OTHER WOMAN by Ann O'Leary. 240 pp. Her roguish
way draws women like a magnet.   ISBN 1-56280-234-8   11.95

SILVER THREADS by Lyn Denison.208 pp. Finding her way
back to love . . .   ISBN 1-56280-231-3   11.95

CHIMNEY ROCK BLUES by Janet McClellan. 224 pp. 4th Tru
North mystery.   ISBN 1-56280-233-X   11.95

OMAHA'S BELL by Penny Hayes. 208 pp. Orphaned Keeley
Delaney woos the lovely Prudence Morris.   ISBN 1-56280-232-1   11.95

SIXTH SENSE by Kate Calloway. 224 pp. 6th Cassidy James
mystery.   ISBN 1-56280-228-3   11.95

DAWN OF THE DANCE by Marianne K. Martin. 224 pp. A dance
with an old friend, nothing more . . . yeah!   ISBN 1-56280-229-1   11.95

WEDDING BELL BLUES by Julia Watts. 240 pp. Love, family,
and a recipe for success.   ISBN 1-56280-230-5   11.95

THOSE WHO WAIT by Peggy J. Herring. 160 pp. Two
sisters . . . in love with the same woman.   ISBN 1-56280-223-2   11.95

WHISPERS IN THE WIND by Frankie J. Jones. 192 pp. "If you
don't want this," she whispered, "all you have to say is 'stop.' "
                                                 ISBN 1-56280-226-7   11.95

WHEN SOME BODY DISAPPEARS by Therese Szymanski.
192 pp. 3rd Brett Higgins mystery.   ISBN 1-56280-227-5   11.95

THE WAY LIFE SHOULD BE by Diana Braund. 240 pp. Which
one will teach her the true meaning of love?   ISBN 1-56280-221-6   11.95

UNTIL THE END by Kaye Davis. 256pp. 3rd Maris Middleton
mystery.   ISBN 1-56280-222-4   11.95

FIFTH WHEEL by Kate Calloway. 224 pp. 5th Cassidy James
mystery.   ISBN 1-56280-218-6   11.95

JUST YESTERDAY by Linda Hill. 176 pp. Reliving all the
passion of yesterday.   ISBN 1-56280-219-4   11.95

THE TOUCH OF YOUR HAND edited by Barbara Grier and
Christine Cassidy. 304 pp. Erotic love stories by Naiad Press
authors.   ISBN 1-56280-220-8   14.95

WINDROW GARDEN by Janet McClellan. 192 pp. They discover
a passion they never dreamed possible.   ISBN 1-56280-216-X   11.95

PAST DUE by Claire McNab. 224 pp. 10th Carol Ashton
mystery.   ISBN 1-56280-217-8   11.95

CHRISTABEL by Laura Adams. 224 pp. Two captive hearts and
the passion that will set them free.   ISBN 1-56280-214-3   11.95

PRIVATE PASSIONS by Laura DeHart Young. 192 pp. An
unforgettable new portrait of lesbian love . . .   ISBN 1-56280-215-1   11.95

BAD MOON RISING by Barbara Johnson. 208 pp. 2nd Colleen
Fitzgerald mystery.   ISBN 1-56280-211-9   11.95

RIVER QUAY by Janet McClellan. 208 pp. 3rd Tru North
mystery.   ISBN 1-56280-212-7   11.95

ENDLESS LOVE by Lisa Shapiro. 272 pp. To believe, once
again, that love can be forever.   ISBN 1-56280-213-5   11.95

FALLEN FROM GRACE by Pat Welch. 256 pp. 6th Helen Black
mystery.   ISBN 1-56280-209-7   11.95

THE NAKED EYE by Catherine Ennis. 208 pp. Her lover in the
camera's eye . . .   ISBN 1-56280-210-0   11.95

OVER THE LINE by Tracey Richardson. 176 pp. 2nd Stevie
Houston mystery.   ISBN 1-56280-202-X   11.95

JULIA'S SONG by Ann O'Leary. 208 pp. Strangely
disturbing . . . strangely exciting.   ISBN 1-56280-197-X   11.95

LOVE IN THE BALANCE by Marianne K. Martin. 256 pp.
Weighing the costs of love . . .   ISBN 1-56280-199-6   11.95

PIECE OF MY HEART by Julia Watts. 208 pp. All the
stuff that dreams are made of —   ISBN 1-56280-206-2   11.95

MAKING UP FOR LOST TIME by Karin Kallmaker. 240 pp.
Nobody does it better . . .   ISBN 1-56280-196-1   11.95

GOLD FEVER by Lyn Denison. 224 pp. By author of *Dream
Lover.*   ISBN 1-56280-201-1   11.95

WHEN THE DEAD SPEAK by Therese Szymanski. 224 pp. 2nd
Brett Higgins mystery.   ISBN 1-56280-198-8   11.95

FOURTH DOWN by Kate Calloway. 240 pp. 4th Cassidy James
mystery.   ISBN 1-56280-205-4   11.95

A MOMENT'S INDISCRETION by Peggy J. Herring. 176 pp.
There's a fine line between love and lust . . .   ISBN 1-56280-194-5   11.95

CITY LIGHTS/COUNTRY CANDLES by Penny Hayes. 208 pp.
About the women she has known . . .   ISBN 1-56280-195-3   11.95

POSSESSIONS by Kaye Davis. 240 pp. 2nd Maris Middleton
mystery.   ISBN 1-56280-192-9   11.95

A QUESTION OF LOVE by Saxon Bennett. 208 pp. Every
woman is granted one great love.   ISBN 1-56280-205-4   11.95

RHYTHM TIDE by Frankie J. Jones. 160 pp.   . . . to desire
passionately and be passionately desired.   ISBN 1-56280-189-9   11.95

PENN VALLEY PHOENIX by Janet McClellan. 208 pp. 2nd
Tru North Mystery.   ISBN 1-56280-200-3   11.95

BY RESERVATION ONLY by Jackie Calhoun. 240 pp. A
chance for true happiness.   ISBN 1-56280-191-0   11.95

OLD BLACK MAGIC by Jaye Maiman. 272 pp. 9th Robin
Miller mystery. ISBN 1-56280-175-9 11.95

LEGACY OF LOVE by Marianne K. Martin. 240 pp. Women
will do anything for her . . . ISBN 1-56280-184-8 11.95

LETTING GO by Ann O'Leary. 160 pp. Laura, at 39, in love
with 23-year-old Kate. ISBN 1-56280-183-X 11.95

LADY BE GOOD edited by Barbara Grier and Christine Cassidy.
288 pp. Erotic stories by Naiad Press authors. ISBN 1-56280-180-5 14.95

CHAIN LETTER by Claire McNab. 288 pp. 9th Carol Ashton
mystery. ISBN 1-56280-181-3 11.95

NIGHT VISION by Laura Adams. 256 pp. Erotic fantasy romance
by "famous" author. ISBN 1-56280-182-1 11.95

SEA TO SHINING SEA by Lisa Shapiro. 256 pp. Unable to resist
the raging passion . . . ISBN 1-56280-177-5 11.95

THIRD DEGREE by Kate Calloway. 224 pp. 3rd Cassidy James
mystery. ISBN 1-56280-185-6 11.95

WHEN THE DANCING STOPS by Therese Szymanski. 272 pp.
1st Brett Higgins mystery. ISBN 1-56280-186-4 11.95

PHASES OF THE MOON by Julia Watts. 192 pp. . . . . hungry
for everything life has to offer. ISBN 1-56280-176-7 11.95

BABY IT'S COLD by Jaye Maiman. 256 pp. 5th Robin Miller
mystery. ISBN 1-56280-156-2 10.95

CLASS REUNION by Linda Hill. 176 pp. The girl from her
past . . . ISBN 1-56280-178-3 11.95

DREAM LOVER by Lyn Denison. 224 pp. A soft, sensuous,
romantic fantasy. ISBN 1-56280-173-1 11.95

FORTY LOVE by Diana Simmonds. 288 pp. Joyous, heart-
warming romance. ISBN 1-56280-171-6 11.95

IN THE MOOD by Robbi Sommers. 160 pp. The queen of
erotic tension! ISBN 1-56280-172-4 11.95

SWIMMING CAT COVE by Lauren Douglas. 192 pp. 2nd
Allison O'Neil Mystery. ISBN 1-56280-168-6 11.95

THE LOVING LESBIAN by Claire McNab and Sharon Gedan.
240 pp. Explore the experiences that make lesbian love unique.
ISBN 1-56280-169-4 14.95

COURTED by Celia Cohen. 160 pp. Sparkling romantic
encounter. ISBN 1-56280-166-X 11.95

SEASONS OF THE HEART by Jackie Calhoun. 240 pp. Romance
through the years. ISBN 1-56280-167-8 11.95

K. C. BOMBER by Janet McClellan. 208 pp. 1st Tru North
mystery. ISBN 1-56280-157-0 11.95

LAST RITES by Tracey Richardson. 192 pp. 1st Stevie Houston mystery. ISBN 1-56280-164-3   11.95

EMBRACE IN MOTION by Karin Kallmaker. 256 pp. A whirlwind love affair. ISBN 1-56280-165-1   11.95

HOT CHECK by Peggy J. Herring. 192 pp. Will workaholic Alice fall for guitarist Ricky? ISBN 1-56280-163-5   11.95

OLD TIES by Saxon Bennett. 176 pp. Can Cleo surrender to a passionate new love? ISBN 1-56280-159-7   11.95

LOVE ON THE LINE by Laura DeHart Young. 176 pp. Will Stef win Kay's heart? ISBN 1-56280-162-7   11.95

DEVIL'S LEG CROSSING by Kaye Davis. 192 pp. 1st Maris Middleton mystery. ISBN 1-56280-158-9   11.95

COSTA BRAVA by Marta Balletbo Coll. 144 pp. Read the book, see the movie! ISBN 1-56280-153-8   11.95

MEETING MAGDALENE & OTHER STORIES by Marilyn Freeman. 144 pp. Read the book, see the movie! ISBN 1-56280-170-8   11.95

SECOND FIDDLE by Kate 208 pp. 2nd P.I. Cassidy James mystery. ISBN 1-56280-169-6   11.95

LAUREL by Isabel Miller. 128 pp. By the author of the beloved *Patience and Sarah*. ISBN 1-56280-146-5   10.95

LOVE OR MONEY by Jackie Calhoun. 240 pp. The romance of real life. ISBN 1-56280-147-3   10.95

SMOKE AND MIRRORS by Pat Welch. 224 pp. 5th Helen Black Mystery. ISBN 1-56280 143-0   10.95

DANCING IN THE DARK edited by Barbara Grier & Christine Cassidy. 272 pp. Erotic love stories by Naiad Press authors. ISBN 1-56280-144-9   14.95

TIME AND TIME AGAIN by Catherine Ennis. 176 pp. Passionate love affair. ISBN 1-56280-145-7   10.95

PAXTON COURT by Diane Salvatore. 256 pp. Erotic and wickedly funny contemporary tale about the business of learning to live together. ISBN 1-56280-114-7   10.95

INNER CIRCLE by Claire McNab. 208 pp. 8th Carol Ashton Mystery. ISBN 1-56280-135-X   11.95

LESBIAN SEX: AN ORAL HISTORY by Susan Johnson. 240 pp. Need we say more? ISBN 1-56280-142-2   14.95

WILD THINGS by Karin Kallmaker. 240 pp. By the undisputed mistress of lesbian romance. ISBN 1-56280-139-2   11.95

THE GIRL NEXT DOOR by Mindy Kaplan. 208 pp. Just what you d expect. ISBN 1-56280-140-6   11.95

NOW AND THEN by Penny Hayes. 240 pp. Romance on the
westward journey. ISBN 1-56280-121-X 11.95

HEART ON FIRE by Diana Simmonds. 176 pp. The romantic and
erotic rival of *Curious Wine.* ISBN 1-56280-152-X 11.95

DEATH AT LAVENDER BAY by Lauren Wright Douglas. 208 pp.
1st Allison O'Neil Mystery. ISBN 1-56280-085-X 11.95

YES I SAID YES I WILL by Judith McDaniel. 272 pp. Hot
romance by famous author. ISBN 1-56280-138-4 11.95

FORBIDDEN FIRES by Margaret C. Anderson. Edited by Mathilda
Hills. 176 pp. Famous author's "unpublished" Lesbian romance.
ISBN 1-56280-123-6 21.95

SIDE TRACKS by Teresa Stores. 160 pp. Gender-bending
Lesbians on the road. ISBN 1-56280-122-8 10.95

WILDWOOD FLOWERS by Julia Watts. 208 pp. Hilarious and
heart-warming tale of true love. ISBN 1-56280-127-9 10.95

NEVER SAY NEVER by Linda Hill. 224 pp. Rule #1: Never get
involved with . . . ISBN 1-56280-126-0 11.95

THE WISH LIST by Saxon Bennett. 192 pp. Romance through
the years. ISBN 1-56280-125-2 10.95

OUT OF THE NIGHT by Kris Bruyer. 192 pp. Spine-tingling
thriller. ISBN 1-56280-120-1 10.95

LOVE'S HARVEST by Peggy J. Herring. 176 pp. by the author of
Once More With Feeling. ISBN 1-56280-117-1 10.95

FAMILY SECRETS by Laura DeHart Young. 208 pp. Enthralling
romance and suspense. ISBN 1-56280-119-8 10.95

INLAND PASSAGE by Jane Rule. 288 pp. Tales exploring conven-
tional & unconventional relationships. ISBN 0-930044-56-8 10.95

DOUBLE BLUFF by Claire McNab. 208 pp. 7th Carol Ashton
Mystery. ISBN 1-56280-096-5 10.95

BAR GIRLS by Lauran Hoffman. 176 pp. See the movie, read
the book! ISBN 1-56280-115-5 10.95

THE FIRST TIME EVER edited by Barbara Grier & Christine
Cassidy. 272 pp. Love stories by Naiad Press authors.
ISBN 1-56280-086-8 14.95

MISS PETTIBONE AND MISS McGRAW by Brenda Weathers.
208 pp. A charming ghostly love story. ISBN 1-56280-151-1 10.95

CHANGES by Jackie Calhoun. 208 pp. Involved romance and
relationships. ISBN 1-56280-083-3 10.95

FAIR PLAY by Rose Beecham. 256 pp. An Amanda Valentine
Mystery. ISBN 1-56280-081-7 10.95

PAYBACK by Celia Cohen. 176 pp. A gripping thriller of romance,
revenge and betrayal. ISBN 1-56280-084-1 10.95

THE BEACH AFFAIR by Barbara Johnson. 224 pp. Sizzling
summer romance/mystery/intrigue.   ISBN 1-56280-090-6   10.95

GETTING THERE by Robbi Sommers. 192 pp. Nobody does it
like Robbi!   ISBN 1-56280-099-X   10.95

FINAL CUT by Lisa Haddock. 208 pp. 2nd Carmen Ramirez
Mystery.   ISBN 1-56280-088-4   10.95

FLASHPOINT by Katherine V. Forrest. 256 pp. A Lesbian
blockbuster!   ISBN 1-56280-079-5   10.95

CLAIRE OF THE MOON by Nicole Conn. Audio Book —
Read by Marianne Hyatt.   ISBN 1-56280-113-9   16.95

FOR LOVE AND FOR LIFE: INTIMATE PORTRAITS OF
LESBIAN COUPLES by Susan Johnson. 224 pp.
    ISBN 1-56280-091-4   14.95

DEVOTION by Mindy Kaplan. 192 pp. See the movie — read
the book!   ISBN 1-56280-093-0   10.95

SOMEONE TO WATCH by Jaye Maiman. 272 pp. 4th Robin
Miller Mystery.   ISBN 1-56280-095-7   10.95

GREENER THAN GRASS by Jennifer Fulton. 208 pp. A young
woman — a stranger in her bed.   ISBN 1-56280-092-2   10.95

TRAVELS WITH DIANA HUNTER by Regine Sands. Erotic
lesbian romp. Audio Book (2 cassettes)   ISBN 1-56280-107-4   16.95

CABIN FEVER by Carol Schmidt. 256 pp. Sizzling suspense
and passion.   ISBN 1-56280-089-1   10.95

THERE WILL BE NO GOODBYES by Laura DeHart Young. 192
pp. Romantic love, strength, and friendship.   ISBN 1-56280-103-1   10.95

FAULTLINE by Sheila Ortiz Taylor. 144 pp. Joyous comic
lesbian novel.   ISBN 1-56280-108-2   9.95

OPEN HOUSE by Pat Welch. 176 pp. 4th Helen Black Mystery.
    ISBN 1-56280-102-3   10.95

ONCE MORE WITH FEELING by Peggy J. Herring. 240 pp.
Lighthearted, loving romantic adventure.   ISBN 1-56280-089-2   11.95

WHISPERS by Kris Bruyer. 176 pp. Romantic ghost story.
    ISBN 1-56280-082-5   10.95

NIGHT SONGS by Penny Mickelbury. 224 pp. 2nd Gianna
Maglione Mystery.   ISBN 1-56280-097-3   10.95

GETTING TO THE POINT by Teresa Stores. 256 pp. Classic
southern Lesbian novel.   ISBN 1-56280-100-7   10.95

PAINTED MOON by Karin Kallmaker. 224 pp. Delicious
Kallmaker romance.   ISBN 1-56280-075-2   11.95

THE MYSTERIOUS NAIAD edited by Katherine V. Forrest &
Barbara Grier. 320 pp. Love stories by Naiad Press authors.
    ISBN 1-56280-074-4   14.95

GOBLIN MARKET by Lauren Wright Douglas. 240pp. 5th Caitlin
Reece Mystery. ISBN 1-56280-047-7 10.95

FRIENDS AND LOVERS by Jackie Calhoun. 224 pp. Mid-
western Lesbian lives and loves. ISBN 1-56280-041-8 11.95

BEHIND CLOSED DOORS by Robbi Sommers. 192 pp. Hot,
erotic short stories. ISBN 1-56280-039-6 11.95

CLAIRE OF THE MOON by Nicole Conn. 192 pp. See the
movie — read the book! ISBN 1-56280-038-8 11.95

SILENT HEART by Claire McNab. 192 pp. Exotic Lesbian
romance. ISBN 1-56280-036-1 11.95

THE SPY IN QUESTION by Amanda Kyle Williams. 256 pp.
A Madison McGuire Mystery. ISBN 1-56280-037-X 9.95

SAVING GRACE by Jennifer Fulton. 240 pp. Adventure and
romantic entanglement. ISBN 1-56280-051-5 11.95

CURIOUS WINE by Katherine V. Forrest. 176 pp. Tenth Anniver-
sary Edition. The most popular contemporary Lesbian love story.
ISBN 1-56280-053-1 11.95
Audio Book (2 cassettes) ISBN 1-56280-105-8 16.95

CHAUTAUQUA by Catherine Ennis. 192 pp. Exciting, romantic
adventure. ISBN 1-56280-032-9 9.95

A PROPER BURIAL by Pat Welch. 192 pp. 3rd Helen Black
Mystery. ISBN 1-56280-033-7 9.95

SILVERLAKE HEAT: A Novel of Suspense by Carol Schmidt.
240 pp. Rhonda is as hot as Laney's dreams. ISBN 1-56280-031-0 9.95

LOVE, ZENA BETH by Diane Salvatore. 224 pp. The most talked
about lesbian novel of the nineties! ISBN 1-56280-030-2 10.95

A DOORYARD FULL OF FLOWERS by Isabel Miller. 160 pp.
Stories incl. 2 sequels to *Patience and Sarah*. ISBN 1-56280-029-9 9.95

MURDER BY TRADITION by Katherine V. Forrest. 288 pp. 4th
Kate Delafield Mystery. ISBN 1-56280-002-7 11.95

THE EROTIC NAIAD edited by Katherine V. Forrest & Barbara
Grier. 224 pp. Love stories by Naiad Press authors.
ISBN 1-56280-026-4 14.95

DEAD CERTAIN by Claire McNab. 224 pp. 5th Carol Ashton
Mystery. ISBN 1-56280-027-2 9.95

CRAZY FOR LOVING by Jaye Maiman. 320 pp. 2nd Robin Miller
Mystery. ISBN 1-56280-025-6 11.95

UNCERTAIN COMPANIONS by Robbi Sommers. 204 pp.
Steamy, erotic novel. ISBN 1-56280-017-5 11.95

A TIGER'S HEART by Lauren W. Douglas. 240 pp. 4th Caitlin
Reece Mystery. ISBN 1-56280-018-3 9.95

PAPERBACK ROMANCE by Karin Kallmaker. 256 pp. A
delicious romance.   ISBN 1-56280-019-1   10.95

THE LAVENDER HOUSE MURDER by Nikki Baker. 224 pp.
2nd Virginia Kelly Mystery.   ISBN 1-56280-012-4   9.95

PASSION BAY by Jennifer Fulton. 224 pp. Passionate romance,
virgin beaches, tropical skies.   ISBN 1-56280-028-0   10.95

STICKS AND STONES by Jackie Calhoun. 208 pp. Contemporary
lesbian lives and loves.   ISBN 1-56280-020-5   9.95
Audio Book (2 cassettes)   ISBN 1-56280-106-6   16.95

UNDER THE SOUTHERN CROSS by Claire McNab. 192 pp.
Romantic nights Down Under.   ISBN 1-56280-011-6   11.95

GRASSY FLATS by Penny Hayes. 256 pp. Lesbian romance in
the '30s.   ISBN 1-56280-010-8   9.95

THE END OF APRIL by Penny Sumner. 240 pp. 1st Victoria
Cross Mystery.   ISBN 1-56280-007-8   8.95

KISS AND TELL by Robbi Sommers. 192 pp. Scorching stories
by the author of *Pleasures*.   ISBN 1-56280-005-1   11.95

STILL WATERS by Pat Welch. 208 pp. 2nd Helen Black Mystery.
                                      ISBN 0-941483-97-5   9.95

TO LOVE AGAIN by Evelyn Kennedy. 208 pp. Wildly romantic
love story.   ISBN 0-941483-85-1   11.95

IN THE GAME by Nikki Baker. 192 pp. 1st Virginia Kelly
Mystery.   ISBN 1-56280-004-3   9.95

STRANDED by Camarin Grae. 320 pp. Entertaining, riveting
adventure.   ISBN 0-941483-99-1   9.95

THE DAUGHTERS OF ARTEMIS by Lauren Wright Douglas.
240 pp. 3rd Caitlin Reece Mystery.   ISBN 0-941483-95-9   9.95

CLEARWATER by Catherine Ennis. 176 pp. Romantic secrets
of a small Louisiana town.   ISBN 0-941483-65-7   8.95

THE HALLELUJAH MURDERS by Dorothy Tell. 176 pp. 2nd
Poppy Dillworth Mystery.   ISBN 0-941483-88-6   8.95

BENEDICTION by Diane Salvatore. 272 pp. Striking, contemporary romantic novel.   ISBN 0-941483-90-8   11.95

COP OUT by Claire McNab. 208 pp. 4th Carol Ashton Mystery.
                                      ISBN 0-941483-84-3   10.95

THE BEVERLY MALIBU by Katherine V. Forrest. 288 pp. 3rd
Kate Delafield Mystery.   ISBN 0-941483-48-7   11.95

THE PROVIDENCE FILE by Amanda Kyle Williams. 256 pp.
A Madison McGuire Mystery.   ISBN 0-941483-92-4   8.95

I LEFT MY HEART by Jaye Maiman. 320 pp. 1st Robin Miller
Mystery.   ISBN 0-941483-72-X   11.95

THE PRICE OF SALT by Patricia Highsmith (writing as Claire
Morgan). 288 pp. Classic lesbian novel, first issued in 1952 . . .
acknowledged by its author under her own, very famous, name.
ISBN 1-56280-003-5   11.95

SIDE BY SIDE by Isabel Miller. 256 pp. From beloved author of
Patience and Sarah.   ISBN 0-941483-77-0   10.95

STAYING POWER: LONG TERM LESBIAN COUPLES by
Susan E. Johnson. 352 pp. Joys of coupledom. ISBN 0-941-483-75-4   14.95

SLICK by Camarin Grae. 304 pp. Exotic, erotic adventure.
ISBN 0-941483-74-6   9.95

NINTH LIFE by Lauren Wright Douglas. 256 pp. 2nd Caitlin
Reece Mystery.   ISBN 0-941483-50-9   9.95

PLAYERS by Robbi Sommers. 192 pp. Sizzling, erotic novel.
ISBN 0-941483-73-8   9.95

MURDER AT RED ROOK RANCH by Dorothy Tell. 224 pp.
1st Poppy Dillworth Mystery.   ISBN 0-941483-80-0   8.95

A ROOM FULL OF WOMEN by Elisabeth Nonas. 256 pp.
Contemporary Lesbian lives.   ISBN 0-941483-69-X   9.95

THEME FOR DIVERSE INSTRUMENTS by Jane Rule. 208 pp.
Powerful romantic lesbian stories.   ISBN 0-941483-63-0   8.95

CLUB 12 by Amanda Kyle Williams. 288 pp. Espionage thriller
featuring a lesbian agent!   ISBN 0-941483-64-9   9.95

DEATH DOWN UNDER by Claire McNab. 240 pp. 3rd Carol
Ashton Mystery.   ISBN 0-941483-39-8   11.95

MONTANA FEATHERS by Penny Hayes. 256 pp. Vivian and
Elizabeth find love in frontier Montana.   ISBN 0-941483-61-4   9.95

THERE'S SOMETHING I'VE BEEN MEANING TO TELL YOU
Ed. by Loralee MacPike. 288 pp. Gay men and lesbians coming out
to their children.   ISBN 0-941483-44-4   9.95

LIFTING BELLY by Gertrude Stein. Ed. by Rebecca Mark. 104 pp.
Erotic poetry.   ISBN 0-941483-51-7   10.95

AFTER THE FIRE by Jane Rule. 256 pp. Warm, human novel by
this incomparable author.   ISBN 0-941483-45-2   8.95

PLEASURES by Robbi Sommers. 204 pp. Unprecedented
eroticism.   ISBN 0-941483-49-5   11.95

These are just a few of the many Naiad Press titles — we are the oldest and
largest lesbian/feminist publishing company in the world. We also offer an
enormous selection of lesbian video products. Please request a complete
catalog. We offer personal service; we encourage and welcome direct mail
orders from individuals who have limited access to bookstores carrying our
publications.

LOOKING FOR NAIAD?

Buy our books at
www.naiadpress.com

or call our toll-free number
1-800-533-1973

or by fax (24 hours a day)
1-850-539-9731